Condition Purple

Also by Peter Turnbull:

Two Way Cut
The Claws of the Gryphon
Big Money
Fair Friday
Dead Knock
Deep and Crisp and Even

PETER TURNBULL

Condition Purple

St. Martin's Press
New York

Library of Congress Cataloging-in-Publication Data
Turnbull, Peter.
      Condition purple / Peter Turnbull.
          p.   cm.
     ISBN 0-312-02892-X
     I. Title.
  PR6070.U68C66   1989
  823'.914—dc19   89-4103
                                                      CIP

First published in Great Britain by William Collins Sons & Co., Ltd.
First U.S. Edition
10 9 8 7 6 5 4 3 2 1

Condition Purple

CHAPTER 1

Tuesday, 17.00–23.40 hours

It is the city of Glasgow, in the grid system at her centre, Victorian buildings standing four square and solid on the hill, going up and then down the other side. It is the evening, the height of summer, and a young woman in heels is walking.

Click. Click. Click. Click.

The young woman is frightened of the evening. She is longing for the night to come, she is longing for the darkness which she can clutch to her like a comfort blanket.

Click. Click.

The man who will kill her when he sees her is in the city. He's on the town. Somewhere. She knows this because she has seen his car cruising in the system, criss-crossing the street.

The woman stops walking and stands at the entrance to the alley, just below Blythswood Square. She has short cropped black hair, a short tight skirt and a black handbag slung over her shoulder.

She knows that the man knows where to find her because she always stands here, at the entrance to West George Lane, off Blythswood Street, looking up and across the road at the National Westminster Bank on the corner of the Square, or looking down the hill to the bus station where the real goats work. The woman stands at the entrance to the alley from 5.30 each evening until midnight, getting into cars and getting out again.

The woman is just twenty-one years old. She is a sister of mercy and she knows that tonight the man will kill her.

She was found at 10.00 p.m., the knife still embedded in her throat. She was found close to where she normally stood, further down the alley, in a crumpled bloody heap under the wall, clearly visible from the street. Twenty minutes after a passing member of the public had glanced along the alley as she passed, and had then raised the alarm, a screen had been placed around the body and two cops stood at either entrance to the alley, to West George Lane: the locus of the offence. Dr Chan, the duty police surgeon, knelt by the body. He had felt for a pulse, had opened the eyes and then pressed them closed again, placed a thermometer in the young woman's mouth and let it remain there for a minute before retrieving it. He then held it up and read the mercury level with the aid of the beam from his pencil torch. He stood and turned to Donoghue.

'Dead,' he said.

Donoghue noted the time. 22.23. 'Stab wounds, I suppose, sir?' he said.

'That is the immediate indication.' Dr Chan was small, dark-haired, wore glasses. 'Though of course that is for the pathologist to verify. The wounds could have been occasioned after death, though in this case I think that that is not likely. The body has all the appearances of having been set on in a most hurried and murderous attack.'

'I'd be inclined to agree.' Donoghue took his pipe with its slightly curved stem from his pocket and placed it in his mouth. He played the flame from his gold-plated lighter across the bowl of the pipe and the sweet aroma of Dutch tobacco began to fill the still evening air. Donoghue looked about him. The alley was long, about three hundred yards from Blythswood Street to West Campbell Street, the distance of one block. The alley itself was part of the alley system in this area of the city; behind each major thoroughfare there is an alley running parallel to it. In this case, Donoghue noted, the alley runs parallel to West George Street. Beginning at Holland Street, it intersects Pitt Street,

Douglas Street, Blythswood Street, West Campbell Street, Wellington Street, Hope Street and ends at Renfield Street. It is about twelve feet wide, mainly cobbled surfaces, and along its length are the rear doors of offices and insurance companies, small indented parking spaces for directors' cars, loading bays, down pipes, windows covered with grilles. The buildings which back on to the alley seemed to Donoghue to be wholly commercial concerns which empty at 6.00 p.m. each night. Occasionally people work as late as 10.00 p.m. There might, thought Donoghue, hoped Donoghue, there might be a building with a resident porter.

He also noticed that the building immediately opposite the wall underneath which the dead woman was found was being rebuilt. So far as he could see in the fading light, the original Victorian edifice was being retained and a new building was being built behind it. Directly opposite the girl wasn't another wall but a row of yellow panels, forming a wooden wall ten feet high.

There might, he thought, be a watchman who could have seen or heard something. He continued to scan the rear of the buildings. Many had lights still burning but he could detect no sign of life from within. The burning lights were nothing more than a sensible burglar deterrent.

Donoghue glanced over the top of the screen and looked at the corpse. She seemed to him to have a hard or a 'used' face, but was by no means unattractive. She had a pleasing figure, long slender legs, and a knife in her throat. She seemed to Donoghue to be in her mid-twenties, but could well be much younger, the girls who work the streets around Blythswood Square age quickly. He knew that. She had died beneath a wall in an alley with the lights of an insurance company building glowing above her.

'I'd like to remain here at the locus and observe the pathologist's work.' Chan spoke to Donoghue, bringing him back to the immediate matter of correct observation procedure. 'If of course you have no objection, Inspector?'

'None whatsoever,' said Donoghue. 'None at all, sir, though the final decision rests with the pathologist, of course.'

'Of course.'

Donoghue liked Dr Chan. He found him polite, quiet, efficient, and in this case he was demonstrating professional interest. Many other police surgeons would be only too anxious to quit the scene of the offence as soon as they had pronounced death. But not Dr Chan. He had often before waited at the scene of the crime in order to observe a kindred professional at work. 'No objection at all, sir,' Donoghue repeated.

Pulling gently and with satisfaction on his pipe, Donoghue walked to the end of the alley, the end of the alley which joins Blythswood Street, the end of the alley from where the passer-by, still shaken, and at that moment still sitting in the rear of the first police vehicle to arrive at the scene, had noticed the folded-up legs of the deceased. The passer-by, a female, upon seeing the body had then apparently ran up to the Square and down to Pitt Street and the Headquarters of the Strathclyde Police, she had burst in through the glass doors and panted, 'Murder, murder,' at the startled commissionaire and had continued to pant, 'Murder, murder, murder,' until calmed by the duty constable. Tango Delta Foxtrot had been ordered to investigate and moments later radioed back a confirmation of an apparent Code 41. The member of the public was escorted to the scene of the crime, but remained in the rear of the area car, giving a statement to Detective-Constable King.

Donoghue approached the car and knelt by the driver's door. Richard King wound down the window.

''Evening, sir,' said King.

'Good evening,' said Donoghue. 'Dr Chan has pronounced the girl dead, Richard. Could you radio control and ask for the services of Dr Reynolds as soon as you like, please.'

'Yes, sir,' Richard King said quickly, precisely. He

reached for the radio microphone and pressed the 'send' button.

Donoghue glanced at the woman in the rear seat of the car. She was young, white-faced and still shaken, her face illuminated at brief one-second intervals by the flashing of the blue light on the roof of the adjacent police vehicle.

The police actively attracted attention. Cars slowed as they passed; a group of women, mostly in short skirts, though one wore jeans and another had a full length fur coat, stood in a cluster at the corner of Blythswood Square.

'Do all the girls wear skirts?' Donoghue asked of the woman in the rear of the patrol car. She had the same hard look that he had noticed about the deceased.

'Aye,' said the woman. 'Some girls wear jeans. Shows the figure off better. Clients like to know what they are getting.'

'I see.'

'This is Diana McLeod,' Richard King said to Donoghue. 'It was Miss McLeod who found the deceased and whom she has identified as one Stephanie Craigellachie.'

'Stephanie Craigellachie,' Donoghue repeated.

'Believed to be twenty-one years of age.'

'Just twenty-one.' Donoghue took his pipe from his mouth. 'I thought she was older.'

'Not according to Miss McLeod, sir,' said King, bearded, chubby, twenty-five-year-old cop.

'We get old in this game,' said Miss McLeod, speaking softly from the rear seat.

'How well did you know the deceased?' Donoghue addressed the woman. King remained silent.

'Just someone to say hello to,' said Diana McLeod. 'No more than that.'

'So what happened tonight?'

'I already told this cop, I mean gentleman.'

'So tell this cop,' said Donoghue.

'Look, I'm a working girl. Time is money.'

'You're doing a public service.'

'We do, to be honest,' said Diana McLeod. 'Basically that's what we do. We keep marriages together, and things.'

'Just tell me what happened, please.' Donoghue allowed a note of impatience to creep into his voice.

'It was about ten o'clock. Getting dark, about that time. I got dropped off in the Square, I'd been servicing a client and he dropped me off in the Square. I began to walk down the hill to my pitch. I passed the alley. I didn't see Stephanie, so I thought she was working . . .'

'Servicing a client?' Donoghue echoed.

'Yes. That's what I thought. I walked down the hill to my pitch. I used to be up nearer the Square, but . . . well, you move with the times, or time moves you, but I'm still a long way from having to stand down by the bus station . . .'

'Just tell me what happened tonight, please.'

'Well, I saw Stephanie wasn't there so I didn't think nothing about it, but I just glanced up the alley, it was light enough to see along it and there were lights from the offices and that, and I saw a pair of legs sticking out of a black mound. I went up and saw it was Stephanie all bloody with a knife in her throat, so I ran to Pitt Street and told the polis. Holy Mary, I never want to see nothing like that again.'

'You got an address where we can reach you, Diana?' King half turned and spoke to the woman.

Diana McLeod gave an address in Garthamlock.

'Bonny Suburbia,' said King, scribbling the information into his notebook.

'Hardly,' she said. 'Not if you know it.'

King did. Low rise, square blocks, concrete, brick and pebbledash, and glass. Lots of glass.

'I've got a three apartment and a couple of kids. My man walked out on me, that's why I'm doing this.'

'Who's watching your kids?'

'My mother. She thinks I've got a job in a night-club. I

don't miss my man, he used to give me terrible doings. See, doing what I do you get treated like a lump of horse meat, but the punters treat me better than my man ever did. There's some real gentlemen about.'

Donoghue noticed a silver Volvo Estate turn off the Square and slow to a stop behind the police vehicle. Dr Reynolds had arrived quickly on the scene. He turned his attention back to the woman. 'If you'd continue to give your statement to this officer, please,' he said. 'It may be that we'll have to visit you at home if we have to clarify a point or two.'

'Well, anything to help, only . . .'

'Yes?'

'See, if you do have to come out to where I stay, you'll be careful what you say in front of my kids and my mother, aye?'

'Aye,' said Donoghue, 'we will. If you scratch our back we'll scratch yours.' He left the area car and walked up the steep incline of Blythswood Street to greet the driver of the Volvo.

'Good evening, sir.'

''Evening, Inspector,' said Reynolds, getting out of his car. He was tall and had a striking mane of silver hair which matched the colour of his car with uncanny accuracy. 'What have we got this time? Fortunately I was at the GRI. Not far to come.'

'Young female, sir,' said Donoghue. 'Just here, down the alley. She has apparently been stabbed. The knife is still in her throat.'

'Useful for you?' smiled the pathologist.

'Well, I hope so, sir.' Donoghue walked beside Reynolds. 'We haven't touched anything. Dr Chan has pronounced the girl dead.'

'Chan?' said Reynolds. 'Yes, I know him, I think.'

'He's still at the locus, sir, anxious to observe your work.'

'I am honoured.'

Donoghue halted and let the tall silver-haired pathologist walk the last few feet alone. Dr Chan turned and stood reverently as Reynolds approached. He gave a slight bow of his head and then accepted Reynolds's extended hand. Reynolds stepped over the orange ribbon which had been erected around the body and invited Chan to follow him. Two uniformed cops stood close by the corpse.

Donoghue refilled his pipe and strolled back on to Blythswood Street and up on to the corner of Blythswood Square. He glanced along the imposing edifice of the RAC Club and then along the early Victorian frontage of West George Street on the south side of the Square. Two girls stood on the corner, talking to each other. One had a black leather coat, the second wore a full-length mink. Donoghue watched as a red BMW drew up alongside the two young women. The two females chatted briefly and then the girl in the mink coat walked towards the BMW in an aggressive, purposeful, hip-swaying motion, spoke briefly with the driver and then got into the car. She was driven away, just a blazing pair of tail lights disappearing into the night. Donoghue looked at the gardens in the centre of the Square, fenced off with high wire, landscaped with mature shrubs. In the summer lunch-times office workers sprawled on the grass enjoying lunch in the fresh air; at night the gardens were the living, silent heart of the Square.

The girl in the leather coat stood and looked across the road at Donoghue, who stood on the opposite kerb. He looked at her. Presently she walked across the road towards him, employing the same purposeful hip-swaying walk her friend had used when approaching the BMW. She smiled at him, holding his eyes with hers as she came on. She stopped, standing in front of him.

'Are you looking for business or are you a cop?' she said. She had a deep, husky voice and was to his eye quite attractive. It was easy to see why she could stand at the top end of the street and edge the Diana McLeods down towards the all-enveloping 'graveyard' near the bus station. She also looked young and innocent and had a long way to go before she assumed the hard, used look of the veterans. She had a fresh, alert sparkle in her eyes.

'I'm a cop,' he said. 'You're not afraid that I might book you for opportuning? You took a risk approaching me.'

The girl smiled and shook her head. 'You don't belong to Vice, otherwise I would have recognized you. It's only Vice and constables anxious to get their arrest rates up that lift you for opportuning, I think you've got more important things to do than throw me in the tank. Anyway, I'm sorry to bother you.'

'No bother,' he said. 'Do you work here each night?'

'I gave my details already. I don't see anything.'

'I'm not just talking about tonight.'

'Look, I'm a working girl.'

'I could make you come down to the station and talk to me.' Donoghue pulled gently on his pipe.

'So what do you want to know? You've scared all the men away anyway, all those blue lights.'

'Your friend's doing all right. I mean the girl in the fur coat who just got into the BMW.'

'Sandra, that's Sandra. The guy was one of her regulars. He's a businessman from Birmingham. He comes up to Glasgow most weeks. Phones Sandra when he comes and she keeps herself available for him. She'll be back in an hour. Then she'll maybe do a bit more business, but tonight you guys . . . I reckon it's an early night for most girls tonight. Anyway, Sandra's regular, he makes it in her interest to wait for him. See the fur coat, full-length mink. That's how much it's in her interest to wait for him.'

'She can make that much money?'

The girl nodded and put a long cigarette to her lips and waited for Donoghue to light it for her. Donoghue was a little slow to react, then, mumbling his apologies, produced his lighter and held the flame up to the tip of her cigarette.

The woman inhaled and while doing so rested her hand gently on the back of Donoghue's hand and looked into his eyes. Donoghue snapped the lighter shut and withdrew his hand. She just can't stop, he thought, just can't stop working.

'Easy,' said the woman, who Donoghue guessed was in her mid-twenties, but who could be hiding a few years either way behind skilfully applied make-up and was also benefiting from the night and the soft lights of the Square. 'Sandra could easy make enough to buy a full-length mink in six or seven nights. That's a good week, mind you. And we don't pay no tax. It's all strictly cash, or maybe kind. Like Sandra's coat.'

'That was given to her?'

'Uh-huh.' The woman inhaled the cigarette with a jerky, affected gesture. 'Her regular, the guy in the BMW, he's in the fur trade. He gave it to her. It's slightly defective, in the lining. Some stitching goes wonky for about three inches, that's all, but it's enough to prevent it being retailed so he brings it to her, a wee gift, a freebie, he says, "A wee gift for you, bonny lass," and that's on top of, not instead of.'

'Can't be bad,' he said, though he knew fine well such a state of affairs lasts as long as the man's whim, and never more than a few months, and he also knew the other side of the coin, not just the girls who work the bus station at the bottom of Blythswood Street but the real dogs who stand in Glasgow Green, earn enough to buy a drink and regularly end the night in the casualty ward of the Glasgow Royal Infirmary.

'It's better than working in an office. We do a good service, me and Sandra. Sandra's regular says it keeps his marriage together.'

'That's the second time I've heard that in the space of half an hour,' said Donoghue.

'Well, that's what he says. He can live with his wife so long as he can see Sandra for an hour or two each time he's in Glasgow, which is most weeks. Sandra's just got to be available, she gets a day's notice and she's got to keep herself clean. We get the AIDS test done twice a month. We're both spick and span.'

'At least you were after your last test.'

'We don't take chances. Never without a rubber. You want to do it without a rubber, away down the bottom of the street or get across to Glasgow Green. There's some real animals in the Green.'

'You don't take men home?'

'No way, never, Jim. In cars, in hotel rooms, in guys' flats, down some alley . . .'

'Down some alley,' echoed Donoghue. 'You know where that girl was found tonight?'

'Down the alley, I know. The gossip went up the street like wildfire. A lot of girls went home, or stood on Cadogan Street for the night, but there's difficulty moving in on someone's pitch, and, like I said, if you go down there guys expect you to do it without a rubber.'

'Did you know her?' asked Donoghue. 'The dead girl, did you know her?'

The woman nodded. 'I mean, I knew her to look at. I recognized her, said, "Hi, how you doin'," things like that, if we passed in the night walking on to our pitch; we don't like getting dropped off at our pitch, we like to get dropped a block away, the next customer doesn't like seeing you getting out of other guys' motors, so we tend to walk the last few yards on to the pitch. So if we walked in opposite directions we'd say "Hi". We have to stick together. There's a lot less bitchiness on the street than in many another place of work. We watch out for each other. So I knew her that way. Didn't ken her name, or where she stayed. She was nice to talk to.'

'You didn't watch out for Stephanie Craigellachie tonight?'

'That her name, aye? See, well, I was with a client in a

motor. I know a quiet place in Cowcaddens. I came back and the street was full of blue flashing lights. Don't make me feel guilty. Besides, it's a risky business at times.'

'You think she was killed by a punter, a client?'

'Don't you?'

'Me, I try to keep an open mind,' Donoghue said. 'Do you normally stand where you were standing tonight? On the corner there?'

'No, the police moved us off the Square, trying to improve the city's image. We have to stand in the streets around the Square, so I stand down there on the corner of St Vincent Street. Only tonight there was all the police around, so I stood with Sandra.'

'Waiting for her regular?'

'That's about it. But corners are best. The guys in the cars like us standing on corners because it's not so obvious that they're stopping to give us the once over. They have to slow down to go round corners anyway.'

'That makes sense. So if you normally stand down there, and Stephanie Craigellachie, as we believe her name to be, stood at the entrance to the alley, just below the Square, then you usually stood about a hundred yards apart and you'd see her most nights.'

'Yes. I'd see her every night I was out. I'm not out each night, but each night I was out I'd see her standing there.'

'Had she been operating long?'

'Longer than me. She was standing there when Sandra brought me down to the Square for the first time. I'll never forget that night, I was scared, feart.'

'Did she have any regulars like Sandra's fur trader?'

'Regulars? No, I don't think so.'

'See her get into the same car more than once at all?'

'All cars look alike to me, Jim, 'cept Rolls-Royces. I can tell a Roller a mile off.'

'See yourself in one, do you?'

'Aye. Don't you?'

'Never really thought about it.'

'Well, maybe my profession pays better.'

'Maybe it does,' said Donoghue. 'But I shall retire with dignity.'

'I shall go out with dignity!' said the woman strongly, sharply, sharply enough for Donoghue to realize that the woman possessed a short, a perhaps violent temper.

'Let's stick to talking about Stephanie Craigellachie,' he said. 'So, no regular?'

'No,' said the woman, calm again. 'She seemed to come out at about six p.m. and take her last client at about midnight. Then she'd walk off, or sometimes join the other girls for a blether before going home.'

'Is that what happens?'

'Aye. We stand a good distance from each other, maybe in pairs, but at the end of the night some girls walk up to each other and blether on about how they did money-wise, what happened, maybe warn about a new guy with dangerous ideas. She'd join them, but I don't think she had a special pal or was in a gang, even. Nice girl.'

'You don't join in. I mean, you said "they" and "them"?'

'No. There's just me and Sandra.'

'I see. Anything else you can tell me?'

'Yes.'

Donoghue was expecting her to say 'no'. Her answer chimed like a bell on a still night, utterly disarming in its honesty.

'Go on.'

'See, it was about two weeks ago, I was standing at the corner, just there, it was early evening, so we're talking about maybe six-thirty p.m. That sort of time. I saw Stephanie, if that's her name, walking along the square in front of the RAC Club. She was coming out for the night, so she comes on and crosses the road to where we're standing now, here, just here, and she stops and she catches her breath. I mean, I'm over there and I hear her catch her breath.' The woman tugged on her nail and blew a plume of smoke out of each nostril. 'Soon as she stops dead in her tracks this guy got out of his motor, parked just across there, see how they park nose in to the kerb, it was like that, one of a number of cars, he got out like he was waiting for her, knowing where she always stands. This guy gets out of his motor, he strode up the hill as easy as if he was walking on the flat and you can see for yourself how steep it is. He had good strength in his legs all right. Good strength. He reached Stephanie, grabbed her arm, I mean really grabbed it, I heard her let out this little gasp and he said, "Right, young lady," and marched her down the street, huckled her into his car, backed up and drove away down the hill. Next time I saw her it was two nights later. She had a bruise on her cheek, she wore a silk scarf high round her neck and she had a pair of shades. Dare say they hid bruising, can't have been dolled up like that for no other reason. Dare say he gave her a rare kicking for some reason. Didn't talk to her about it, tho' some of the others might have done, but not me.'

'You don't remember the make of the car?'

'They all look the same to me, Jim.' A sharp pull on the nail accompanied by a jerk of the head. 'All the same, 'cept Rollers.'

'So do you remember the colour?'

'Black.'

'Black,' Donoghue echoed. 'Anything about the car make it stand out at all?'

'Yeah, it had a pair of large fluffy dice hanging from the interior mirror and fancy wheels, and fancy unholstery, like it was tarted up. I think the windscreen was tinted.'

'All right,' said Donoghue, taking a mental note of the details that he would jot down at his earliest convenience. 'The man: he had strong legs. What else did you notice?'

'He was short. I guess about my height, that's five-six, short for a guy.'

'Not in Glasgow.'

'Look, do you want me to help you or don't you?'

'Do you want to continue this discussion down at the police station or not? If we took you down you'd be booked for opportuning, help us keep our arrest rate up. It's up to you.'

'OK. So he was still about five-six. So what?'

'Dress?'

'Smart, what they call casual but smart. Safari jacket, light-coloured trousers, sports shoes, canvas shoes with a good sole, open-neck shirt, gold medallion hanging round his neck. A small wee hunk of a man and he just oozed money. That's why I remember him. I could go a man like that, even if he was just five-six.'

'I dare say you'd go for anyone who's got money.'

'Most anyone.'

'Can I have your name?' Donoghue reached for his notebook and took a pen from his jacket-pocket.

'And my telephone number?' She miled an insincere smile. 'Hazel Tennant.'

'Address, please.'

She gave an address in the Anderston development.

'Couldn't be more convenient for you, could it?'

'Couldn't really, could it? I share it with Sandra. It's a three apartment.'

'Two-bedroomed council flat ten minutes' walk from the Square, good quality housing, and there's whole families living in damp bed-and-breakfast accommodation, all in the one room and a plate of cereal and a cup of tea for breakfast.'

'We had contacts, we gave favours, strings got pulled. It's easy if you know how. Besides, me and Sandra will be off the game in a year or two, we'll have a bought house by then.'

'Did Sandra see that incident?'

'Incident?'

'The five-six guy in the safari jacket who oozed money

and who bundled the soon to be deceased Stephanie Craigel-lachie into his tarted-up motor?'

'Aye, she saw it all right.'

'Good, well you can advise Sandra that a police officer will be calling on her to speak to her about it, to take a statement from her.'

'Is that necessary? I mean, the flat's our wee hidey-hole, she's on the street most nights . . .'

'Both she and you will be run in if you don't stop dictating terms.' Donoghue glanced down Blythswood Street. He could see one or two girls standing a respectable distance from the police activity, people walking past them, men occasionally stopping for a brief exchange, cars clearly cruising slowly. The more he looked, the more he could recognize a whole operation of girls and cruising motors, which he would not notice with a casual glance. 'Police business takes us anywhere at any time, and if an individual is not prepared to make herself available then we will make her available. If you see what I mean.'

'OK, OK.'

Donoghue saw Dr Chan leave the alley and walk to his car. He got in and drove away. The unmistakable tall silver-haired figure of Dr Reynolds followed Dr Chan out of the alley, moving as always at his own pace. He crossed the street to where his car stood, placed the black bag on the rear seat and then strolled up Blythswood Street to where Donoghue waited.

'Good evening, sir,' said Donoghue.

''Evening, 'evening' Inspector.'

'Hi,' said Hazel Tennant, casting a professional eye over a new male. 'You another cop, aye?'

'No, I'm a pathologist.'

'A what?'

'A doctor, I cut up bodies.'

'Stephanie going to get cut up?'

'A word, Inspector.' Reynolds addressed Donoghue and

the two men strolled a few paces away from the prying ears of Hazel Tennant.

'Done all I can here,' said Reynolds. 'I'll have the body removed to the Royal and commence the post mortem immediately.'

'Thank you. Can you give me anything to go on?'

'Well, death certainly seems to have been caused by the single knife wound to the throat. Time of death, well, could be up to six hours ago, that's based on purely clinical observations, but really I can't see the body lying where it is for six hours and not be seen in that time, this is the centre of the city in the summer time for heaven's sake, but that is your department. I'll have her clothing sent on to Forensic Science as soon as possible. Her possessions to you, I presume?'

'Thank you.'

'Have you located the next of kin at all?'

'No,' said Donoghue. 'We're not even certain of her name. She's known as Stephanie Craigellachie, but that could be assumed, sort of "nom de rue" if you see what I mean.'

'I think she was killed where she was found,' said Reynolds. 'There's no hard evidence, but she seems to have slumped where she was found, rather than having been dumped. The body is in the posture I would expect it to be in if it had fallen immediately after the knife thrust to the throat which punctured the venous artery. Some bodies have clearly been dumped, they are found in postures the body could not naturally assume, others have been almost ritualistically laid out. But in this case the deceased seems to have fallen back against the wall and then slumped sideways.'

'I see.'

'Well, I'll be on my way,' said Reynolds, turning towards his car. 'I'll 'phone you with my findings. The report will follow in due course.'

'Again, thank you. If I'm not in the station you can leave a message.'

Donoghue pulled out his hunter and glanced at the face. It was 10.30 p.m. He'd been at work since 8.30 a.m. Nothing new, nothing new to a cop in this city. He'd hand over to a member of the team, then drive home to Edinburgh, to a newly built bungalow, to two sleeping children, to a wife who would register her disappointment at his long hours by pretending to be asleep when he crept into their bedroom. He walked back towards Hazel Tennant. 'Well, like I said, we'll be calling on your friend and you'd perhaps like to think further about the incident, any detail could be vital. We don't like any murder, we especially don't like the murders of young women.'

'Young! She's older than me.'

Donoghue was surprised. 'How old are you?'

'Nineteen,' she said indignantly. 'I was nineteen yester-day.'

The task fell to WPC Willems. She attended at the address on the envelope of a letter which had been posted to Stephanie Craigellachie and which had been found among the possessions of the deceased. The address was that of a flat in Gibson Street, Kelvinbridge. She entered the close, it was old and damp and crumbling, winding tightly. No stair lighting. She switched on her flashlight. The railings were of thin wrought iron and the flagstones had been worn down over the years, and had become displaced here and there as the building had 'settled' or had slid an inch or two down the hill towards the Kelvin. She shone the beam of her torch on the names of the doors as she passed. Many doors had a number of names pinned to them, probably students or unemployed, she thought, living where they can. Other doors had names such as 'Singh' or 'Rafiq'.

At the top of the close, underneath a massive expanse of glass skylight, she came across a dull brown door with the names 'Craigellachie' and 'Spence' written in a neat hand on lined paper and taped to the door.

Elka Willems rapped the door. The echoing of her knocking rang down the close. She hammered on the door a second time. No response. She bent down and looked through the letter-box. The flat was in darkness. It seemed, so far as she could see, to be a cleanly kept flat, a carpet on the floor, pictures on the wall. She called out, 'Hello, police.'

No response.

She rapped the door again. Still no response. She turned to go and then heard a noise, an opening door and a footfall, a creaking floorboard, from within the flat. A light was switched on. A bleary female voice said, 'Who is it?'

'Police.'

The letter-box was pulled open and a pair of eyes blinked at Elka Willems. The letter-box snapped shut and the door was unlocked and pulled wide.

A girl stood in the doorway, about nineteen, twenty, brown eyes, dark curly hair, slightly built body, a dressing-gown, slender legs, bare feet. 'What is it?' she said, yawning.

Half an hour later, when the ashtray on the kitchen table was full of ash and cigarette butts, the girl said she still couldn't believe it, she still couldn't.

'It's always hard,' said Elka Willems.

'Has this happened to you, lost someone you know well?'

'Not yet, but it's part of my job to knock on doors at all hours of the day and night to tell parents and wives and husbands about the sudden death of a member of their family. In the case of Stephanie we still have to do it. But the emotion is something you get used to. The worst ones of all are the ones who just don't take it in, they say, 'Yes, I hear you, but she's coming home soon. She'll be back as usual.' They're the worst of all.'

'I can bet. I couldn't do your job. Wanted to once, mind.'

'Did you?'

'Never put myself forward. I reached five feet two and

stopped growing. I'm always the last one to find out that it's snowing. It is too small, isn't it. Five-two.'

'Yes. It's five-eight for men and five-six for women. They might take you if you're shorter and have really good potential, but not much shorter. So what do you do yourself, Karen?'

Karen Spence shrugged. 'This and that.'

'Been up to the Square yourself?'

'Once or twice when money was tight, two or three nights would buy me a two-week package holiday in Spain if I was fed up, but that's all, I just dabbled in it, played at it. Not like Stephanie, out every night, flung herself into it she did, seven days a week, she's bringing home big money.'

'Where does it go?' Elka Willems looked about her. The flat was neat, but had a 'cheap' feel about it. 'Is she a smack-head?'

'Not that I know of.' Karen Spence lit another cigarette. 'She's not daft, she keeps herself clean as well, no infections, no VD, no AIDS, she's spotless, always uses a rubber and never kisses. She told me, she says you have to keep the transmission of body fluids to a minimum.'

'Very sensible of her.'

'It's a business like any other and it's competitive. She can't, I mean couldn't, go on standing at the top of the street near the Square for ever, so she was making the most of it, I suppose, working hard and keeping herself clean. I think she was planning to retire once she had saved enough, find a good man, settle down, have a couple of kids, one of each. I think that that was what she wanted.'

'What do you know of her background?'

Karen Spence nodded to the six lines of notes Elka Willems had written in her notebook. 'That,' she said. 'Really, I don't know anything else.'

'She came from Bearsden.' Elka Willems glanced at her notebook.

'Yes. She didn't speak much about her background. If

she spoke it tended to be about what sort of night she had
had. She usually came back about midnight, sometimes she
didn't come back until six in the morning, when she was
that late it was because she had been working the casinos.
If she didn't come back at all she had been huckled by the
Vice Squad and thrown in the tank.'

'So we know her, she's got convictions?'

'Opportuning, three counts. She was fined fifty pounds,
then a hundred, then a hundred and fifty. That's small beer.
The total amount of those fines she can earn in a couple of
nights in a good week. The fines are like a small amount of
income tax.'

'Which address did she give when she was bounced into
the van?'

'This one. This is her place of domicile. Incidentally,
bounced is right, some cops in Vice are pure swines, especially the women, once they gave her a thirteen-hour
tank, cooped up in that wee room for thirteen hours with
other women, and once she came home with a sore face.
Of course nobody saw anything, so she couldn't make a
complaint.'

'And nobody saw anything tonight. Street full of girls and
a man takes Stephanie into an alley, just a few feet away
from the street, shoves a knife into her throat and walks
away again and nobody saw or heard anything. You're in
a glass house, hen, so don't toss rocks.'

'I'm not in anything,' said the girl. Elka Willems noticed
a hard look in her eyes. 'But OK, I take your point. I can't
help you any more.'

'I really think that that is for me to decide.'

'She came from Bearsden, she worked the street. If I've
told you once . . .'

'Don't get ratty. We could continue this down at the
station if necessary.'

'It boils down to the same thing. I have nothing else I
can tell you.'

'Did she have a pimp?'

'No.' Karen Spence dragged down the last quarter of an inch of her nail and dogged the tip. 'She told me she got approached by guys from time to time, all girls do. They say, "Have you got anybody looking after you on the street?" and they'll offer to watch their backs for ten per cent of the night's take. She told them to walk half way along the Kingston Bridge and then start walking sideways. She didn't need any pimp.'

'Which is her room?'

The girl nodded to a door which stood behind her. Elka Willems rose from the table and tried the door. It was locked.

'It's locked,' said Karen Spence. 'It always is. Locks it when she goes out. Dare say it makes her feel safe, it's good to have a space of your own, you know, a room, just one ten by ten bolthole where she can be by herself and not violated by anyone. I suppose she needs that room in order to keep working. Her room back here and her spray for the street.'

'Spray?'

'An aerosol of hair lacquer. Keeps it in her handbag. It goes into the eyes of any man who gets too fresh. It stings like hell and gives her the ten seconds she needs to get out of the car.'

'That's where she does it, in cars, aye?'

'Cars, guys' flats, hotel rooms, shop doorways, up a close. You name it, she does it there.'

'But not here.'

'Absolutely not.'

Elka Willems walked to the door of the flat. 'You'll not be going too far, no?'

The girl shook her head.

'We'll probably be wanting to talk to you again.'

'I'll be here. Or up the Square.'

'The Square?'

'The streets around the Square. I mean, there's a vacancy for me now, isn't there.'

Elka Willems glanced at her watch. It was twenty minutes to midnight.

CHAPTER 2

Wednesday, 02.00–07.30 hours

The scene had been acted out before. The set was the same, the props were the same, the principal players were the same. Sussock had seen it all so many times before and it never got easier. It never got easier because the room and the play always said the same thing about human existence: nobody gets out alive, you can maybe, just maybe, complain . about the manner and time of your end. And because of that some scenes were a little, just a little, more difficult than others. They might be bloodier, or quite neat and clean, but yet possessed an overpowering sense of tragedy. Sussock felt that this was just such a scene, it was tragic because the player at the centre of the scene was, or at least had been, young, with her life ahead of her, and because she had not been killed in an accident or by natural causes which no one could be responsible for, but because she had been murdered, for which many people could be responsible, not just the one person who pushed the knife into her venous artery, but those who looked and walked the other way when she needed assistance, or those who didn't respond to her cry for help. A single act of murder, in Sussock's experience, could very often leave blood on many hands.

The room was brilliantly illuminated with twin rows of fluorescent bulbs encased in clear perspex shields which cut out the 'shimmer'. The room was rectangular in shape, three walls were of bare white paint, the fourth side of the

room was delineated by a single sheet of glass, behind which
was a bank of seats in four rows, all at that moment empty.
In the centre of the room was a stainless steel table with a
one inch 'lip' around its edge and supported by a single
hollow pedestal. At the side of the table was a trolley,
also in stainless steel, upon which lay rows of surgical
instruments. The floor of the room was covered with industrial grade linoleum and was heavily sealed with disinfectant. The room was the pathology laboratory in the
basement of the Glasgow Royal Infirmary.

There were four people in the room. Dr Reynolds, tall
and silver-haired, cut as always a striking figure. He calmly
buttoned his white smock while speaking into a minute
microphone which was attached to his lapel. 'Zero two
hundred hours, seventeenth of July . . .' he spoke softly,
unhurriedly. The second person stood beside the trolley. He
was the mortuary assistant who, to Sussock, had always
had a sinister gleam in his eye. He was a small man, even
by the norm for the West of Scotland he was small, the
distinct gleam in his eyes which Sussock always noticed was
the look in the eyes of a man who enjoyed his work in the
most unhealthy manner. Sussock had noticed a similar look
in the eyes of other men, at a sports centre of all places, in
the restaurant where people were milling around, most
wearing tracksuits or maybe blazers and white trousers. In
that scene four men stood out: they too were short in stature,
and like the mortuary attendant had close-cut hair; they
wore city suits and stuck closely together rather than carve
out a large floor area, like the men of the soccer team or the
ladies attending the centre for basket-ball training. Those
four men conveyed a sense of smugness and self-satisfaction
and tended to grin and smile continually at each other.
They were, it transpired, the 'gun club' and their sport was
blowing splinters out of wooden target posts as speedily and
efficiently as possible. Sussock had the impression that, if
given the chance, those four men could blow holes in human

targets with the same speed and efficiency and probably with considerable relish. Whenever Sussock had occasion to attend a post mortem, and whenever he met the mortuary assistant, he was always reminded of the gentlemen of the 'gun club'.

Sussock was the third person in the room. His function was to represent the police as a witness to the post mortem, as a solicitor sometimes does for the defence, and it was his place to be summoned by the pathologist who might have a question to ask or who might say, 'Look, look at this, this is the cause of death.'

The fourth person in the room was the centre of the piece: the leading player. It was the corpse.

Sussock had opened the door of the pathology laboratory to find the attendant close to the corpse. The attendant glanced quickly at Sussock and then sprang back and assumed his usual position beside the instrument trolley. Sussock saw the corpse and sighed. He had been asked by Donoghue to attend a post mortem. 'Female, Ray,' Donoghue had said, reaching for his homburg and pulling on his pipe. 'Down at the GRI. Soon as you like.' Sussock had grabbed his light summer coat and driven across the grid system to the GRI as soon as he liked, reported to the reception area at Casualty, walked out behind the casualty building and across the courtyard surrounded on all sides by the bleak imposing Victorian architecture, and then entered the body of the hospital. Descended the wide flight of stairs and walked along the basement corridor with pipes running along the roof and entered the pathology laboratory in time to see the assistant leap back from the dissecting table. On the table was the body of a young woman. She had a pleasant if somewhat round face, red hair, a real mane of red hair, pleasantly shaped and sized breasts which seemed as she lay there to be well rounded and firm, at least they had been in life, a ribcage, a flat stomach and a trim waist, long slender legs and well proportioned feet with a

good high instep. A towel had been draped over what is
officially termed her 'private parts', and Sussock noticed
that the towel had been carelessly positioned, or had been
recently disturbed. Sussock looked from the corpse to the
assistant, who held his stare and even goaded Sussock with
a slight, almost imperceptible twitch at the lips, just the
beginning of a knowing smile.

Sussock moved to the corner of the room, distancing
himself from the mortuary assistant more than he was
distancing himself from the corpse. Yet his eyes were drawn
to the corpse. Deathly white, it had an artificial look about
it, closer it seemed to Sussock to a store window mannequin
more than to a living and breathing human being. In the
side of the neck was a small but none the less gaping wound.
It was a wound which was highly localized, highly, totally
lethal. The body had been washed down with a disinfectant
solution which added to the all-pervading smell of disinfectant in the room. Sussock wondered whether, if the corpse
of Stephanie Craigellachie had not been washed, he could
by now be smelling her death odour. Sussock was in his
fifty-fifth year and he had been a cop since he left the RAF
after his national service and in that time he had seen many,
many corpses, of men and women, of young and old, and
each had the smell of death and the smell was always the
same, like rotting leaves but a little sweeter and heavier.

Then, as Sussock was pondering, the door of the laboratory burst open with a loud 'click' and Dr Reynolds entered
with a flourish, saying, 'Good morning, good morning,' as
he breezed into the room. He stood by the corpse, buttoned
his smock and spoke into the microphone which was attached to his lapel. 'Zero two hundred hours, seventeenth
of July . . . the post mortem of female Caucasian believed
to be one Stephanie Craigellachie . . .' Reynolds glanced at
Sussock. 'That is the correct name, I take it, Sergeant?'

'I really have no idea, sir.' Sussock raised his voice
sufficiently for it to carry across the floor space. 'I was asked

by Inspector Donoghue to attend here at short notice. I was
just told that it was a female corpse.'

'I see. Well, as it was the good Inspector himself who
provided me with the name, I will use it until otherwise
advised.' Reynolds slipped his hand into the pocket of
his smock, switched on the tape-recorder and repeated
'. . . believed to be one Stephanie Craigellachie, aged approximately twenty years. Immediately apparent is a
wound, apparently a knife wound to the left of the throat.'
Reynolds switched off the recording machine and took an
instrument from the trolley. Sussock thought the instrument
to be no more than a long stainless steel rod with which
Reynolds began probing the wound with the aid of a pencil
beam torch. Then Reynolds stood and looked at Sussock.
'No need to cut up the body any more than is necessary,'
he said.

'Indeed, sir.'

'You see, I think that I can safely say that this wound is
the cause of death, it's deep and narrow and has pierced
the venous artery. The blood would have spurted out and
there was, as I recall, sufficient blood at the locus for us to
assume that she was attacked there.'

'Sir?'

'Well, as I said to Inspector Donoghue, I think the murder
happened in the alley because of the position of the body;
it was slumped against the wall in the manner that it
assumes naturally. I mean that it had not been dumped
leaving the limbs in an unnatural position, nor had it been
laid out.'

'I see, sir.'

'And the amount of blood noted at the locus and on her
clothes is in keeping with the amount of blood I would
expect to have been lost as a result of this injury.'

'So she wasn't killed earlier and at a different location
and carried to the alley,' said Sussock. 'She was attacked
there and her attacker let her lie where she fell.'

'Exactly. If she had been killed by a different method, by poisoning for example, she just wouldn't have bled so much when the artery was punctured. It would have needed a working heart to pump that amount of blood out on to the cobblestones.'

'I see.'

'The other thing that indicates that this wound was the cause of death is that it must have been so obviously fatal. It is a lucky or unlucky wound depending on your point of view, unless of course her attacker was well acquainted with the human body, in which case it is a precisely targeted injury. What I mean is that it may be that the attacker was going to slash her face or stab her chest, she defended herself and in doing so probably deflected the knife. The blood would have gushed out like water from a hose and it must have been obvious to the attacker that he had killed her. Whether he wished to is not certain, but what is certain is that with a single blow her life was snuffed out. The attacker may well have been covered in her blood, particularly the forearm of the hand which held the knife.'

'Can you say anything about the attacker, sir?'

'All in good time, Sergeant. Let's look at the murder weapon first.' Reynolds knelt and took a small plastic sachet from the lower tray of the instrument trolley. The sachet contained a knife, an ordinary kitchen knife so far as Sussock could tell, wooden handle, five-inch blade. Reynolds took the knife from the sachet and held it delicately between thumb and forefinger. He switched on the microphone.

'The murder weapon, so assumed, is a five-inch-bladed kitchen knife,' he said softly. 'It was reported to have been found still embedded in the corpse.' Reynolds measured the width of the wound and slid the knife into the wound itself. 'I find by measuring and testing that the knife provided and seen by me to have been embedded in the corpse fits the wound. My findings are consistent with the knife provided being the murder weapon.' He replaced the knife inside the plastic sachet and handed the sachet to the assistant. 'Seal and label this, please.' Reynolds looked at the wound. 'Now to answer your question, Mr Sussock. The murderer, to occasion this injury which seems to have a downward plane, would probably have a shoulder height a little more than the shoulder height of the victim. West George Lane has an uneven surface, he could be smaller but standing on higher ground at the time of the attack, that way he would have had a distinct height advantage. Now the wound is on the left side of her neck, so if the attacker was facing her he was right-handed. If he came up behind her he could be either left- or right-handed. Can't be of greater help than that, I'm afraid.'

'No matter, sir.'

'Well now, let's look at the corpse and see what she can tell us about herself. Dead people tell many tales. Do you think that she was opportuning, Sergeant?'

'Probably, sir. Time of night, manner of dress, location of attack.'

'Then she's a high risk AIDS carrier,' Reynolds said calmly. Sussock enjoyed seeing the attendant start in sudden fear.

'Yes, she's that all right,' Reynolds continued. 'Diamorphine into both arms, and her neck too by all accounts.'

'Heroin?'

'Heroin,' said Reynolds. 'Do you want to come over here and see for yourself? Don't worry about the virus, we're finding that it's very delicate outside the human body and you can have a lot of tactile contact with an AIDS carrier without placing yourself at risk.' Sussock stepped across the floor.

'See, here,' said Reynolds.

Ray Sussock had seen similar marks on other people's arms and legs and feet before, small pin-pricks running in a wavy line. One by itself could easily be overlooked in all except the most minute examinations, but scores of such marks caused a distinct pattern.

'I'll do the HIV test, it's simple enough and I'll be able to get the result to you very quickly, but even if it's negative, if you go to her place of residence make sure you treat any syringe or other sharp edge with respect.'

'I'll certainly bear that in mind, sir.'

'Well—' Reynolds took the towel reverently from the body—'I don't suppose she'll mind . . .' He folded the towel and placed it neatly and carefully on the trolley, above the head of the corpse. 'Well,' he said again, though this time with a note of surprise, 'what do you make of that?'

Sussock was unsure what to make of what until Reynolds delicately ran his finger on the inside of the girl's left groin, near to where the hem of her underwear would normally rest. There, partially hidden by the edge of the 'V' of her pubic hair, was a tattoo. It read: 'I belong to Dino.'

'I belong to Dino,' said Sussock. 'I'd like to arrange for that to be photographed, sir.'

'Of course. In fact you could do that perhaps, Mr Millard.'

'It would be a pleasure, sir,' said the assistant. Then he smiled once again at Sussock.

'Don't catch anything,' Sussock snarled at Millard. Millard's face fell. Reynolds moved to the foot of the table and placed his hands on the bottom of her legs, close to her feet and gently eased her legs apart. 'Poor girl,' he said.

'Oh?'

'Vaginal warts,' he said. 'Sex could have caused her some discomfort. Not pleasant for any female, but if you've got to do it to buy your heroin, then it must be doubly unpleasant.'

'Indeed,' said Sussock. Heroin, vaginal warts, maybe AIDS, West George Lane at 10.00 p.m., Stephanie Craigel-lachie had everything going for her.

Reynolds grasped both her feet. 'Let's flip her over.' Millard took the shoulders. 'Three . . . two . . .' said

Reynolds and the body of Stephanie Craigellachie was turned on to its anterior plane in a neat, quick, well-practised manœuvre. 'We always do it clockwise,' said Reynolds, noting Sussock's admiration.

It was to Sussock's eyes, had he not been viewing a corpse, a not unattractive view of a young female. Again he found his eyes wandering to the assistant, Millard, and was not disappointed to find the man gazing at the corpse as though it was a feast to be devoured.

Stephanie Craigellachie's back, Sussock noted, was well-proportioned, and muscular rather than weak; her buttocks, he felt, were perhaps a little on the large side for her to have made a career modelling swimwear, but none the less she had in life probably considered herself to have a good figure, which is all that matters. Sussock could see nothing of concern but Reynolds's trained eyes began to pick out minutiæ of evidence. 'Here,' he said, 'here, here, and here,' and began to point to places on the lower curve of the buttocks and upper rear legs of the corpse.

'See them?'

'No, I don't,' said Sussock.

'Small patches of white skin, about a quarter to half an inch long.'

'Oh yes.'

'Old lacerations,' said Reynolds, 'years old. I presume she had an accident, fell on to broken glass or similar. That sort of thing.'

'Oh,' Sussock said. 'Nothing of relevance to her death, then?'

'Nothing at all. I think these injuries were sustained in childhood or adolescence, but I'll mention them in my report anyway. Never know what is and what is not of relevance, but they contributed nothing to her death as such.'

'So,' said Sussock, 'death was due to stabbing, pure and simple?'

'Yes,' Reynolds replied. 'One blow, one penetration.'

'The knife there is the murder weapon?'

'Yes,' said Reynolds, and then: 'Well, the knife could have caused the injury. It's reasonable to assume that it is the murder weapon. Slightly different emphasis. Just to cover myself.'

'The deceased abused heroin?'

'Yes, to quite a marked degree.'

'And she once knew or might still know a person called Dino.'

'Apparently, though I shudder to think of the nature of their relationship.'

'Oh?'

'Well, a tattoo is painful to imprint anywhere on the body, but there, at the top of the leg, at the groin, that is a particularly sensitive area. It would have taken some time to do that and it could have been very painful for her. It could have been an ordeal.'

'Well, it's something to go on,' said Sussock. 'In the absence of anything else to do we can look for Dino.'

'Don't take yourself up a blind alley, the tattoo is some months old. I'll do the HIV test and have the wound and the tattoo photographed.'

'Thank you, sir.' Sussock turned to go. He crossed the floor and opened the door. As he did so, he glanced backwards and saw Reynolds peeling off his surgical gloves and Millard running his eyes lovingly over the body of Stephanie Craigellachie, deceased.

Sussock left the hospital. It was a warm, balmy night with a pleasant breeze blowing from the south-west which whirled round the inner courtyard of the GRI. July. He counted off the months. Maybe he'd get through August, but in Scotland the ground frost can appear in mornings in August and in September the nights could already be cold enough to make his chest pinch. It was the legacy of having been a cigarette-smoker for a major proportion of his adult life. In the winter he suffered; for eight months from September to April the nights, all the nights and many of the days, caused him to have to live with a sharp pain in his chest as the icy air gripped at his lungs. But at the moment, now, it was July, it was warm, his chest didn't hurt; he could even take deep breaths and kid himself that he was healthy.

He walked through the casualty reception area of the GRI. He thought the waiting-room surprisingly full for 3.00 a.m., midweek. People sat in the waiting area, as individuals or in groups, agitated, or in a state of shock with no apparent injury, or holding a bloody towel or bandage to some part of their body. Paper tissues and cardboard vomit bowls littered the floor. No one talked.

He walked out into the summer night again. Out to where he had left his car in the space marked 'Ambulances Only'. Such latitude is excusable at 03.00 hours. A police car had parked behind him, two officers sat inside writing up their notebooks. He didn't recognize them.

Sussock drove across town. The city was at her quietest, a few buses, taxis, refuse collectors following the refuse lorries, the occasional drunk still staggering home. He turned down into George Square. A few younger people still sat on the benches, not wanting to go home, not being bothered by the law, people just waiting for the next all-night bus to an outlying town. Everything quiet, nothing getting out of hand. Hundreds of starlings sat, twittering noisily, on the front of the City Chambers. He drove up Bath Street, a long canyon of Victorian buildings with white lights attached to the buildings rather than standing on poles. He parked his car close to Blythswood Square and to West George Lane. PC Phil Hamilton stood on the entrance to the lane.

''Morning, Sarge.' Sussock stopped close to Hamilton.

'Quieter than normal.' Hamilton rocked backwards and

forwards on his feet. 'I've scared all the action down towards the bus station. The car drivers cruise round the corner, clock me and put their foot down, so the girls have gone to the bottom of the street, for tonight at any rate.'

Sussock glanced down the street and saw a woman standing alone under the spill of a street lamp.

'Just one or two left now,' said Hamilton. 'Earlier on, there was a whole team of them down there. The Vice came round and huckled a few into the van. I think they wanted to be seen to be doing something since they knew we were hanging about, eagle-eyed. Most of the rest drifted off about one or two a.m. The girl down there and one or two others on Holm Street and Cadogan Street, the Vice told me they're waiting for the casinos to shut for night at about five a.m.'

'Long hours,' said Sussock. He knew little about Hamilton. He was a steady cop, wouldn't set the heather on fire, he was about twenty-four, married to a nurse, so he understood.

'Maybe, Sarge, but they can earn big money. Even more than you and me.'

'Even more.' Sussock grinned. Hamilton had a sense of humour. 'Well, they can keep it. Can I borrow your torch a second, please?'

Hamilton handed Sussock his flashlight and Sussock played the beam across the surface of the alley.

Hamilton watched. 'Looking for something, Sarge? We swept it, it's clean.'

'Looking at the blood,' said Sussock, letting the torch-beam dwell on the wide dark stain which covered a large area of the cobbles. 'Aye, there's a lot there right enough. See, I'm just after attending the post mortem, the pathologist said that she could have shed a great deal of blood at the location of the attack. It means that this is the locus of the offence.'

'She wasn't dumped here?'

'That's it.'

'The rats were out earlier,' said Hamilton. 'I chucked some stones at them and they went squealing off.'

'After the blood were they, aye?'

'Aye,' said Hamilton. 'About half a dozen big ones—they get big in the summer, the rats—came up scratching it off the cobbles and licking it. All good food to them, I suppose.'

'I suppose it is,' said Sussock. He thought that in a sense, since Stephanie Craigellachie had been preyed on by rats while alive, it just completed the picture that the night-time gutter rats came scratching up the alley to pick at her dried blood. No, it didn't, it didn't complete the picture at all, it just made the wretched female's life doubly cheap. She was a two-time loser.

He walked on down West George Street, walking round the block to return to his car, enjoying the evening. He walked passed stone-coloured doorways, brass plates and stairs leading up. There was no sound, not on the street, no cars, no buses here, just the soft measured sound of his own footfall. Then a voice in darkness said, 'Looking for business?' He turned. At the top of a flight of stairs was a girl in a long summer dress which seemed to be of suede patchwork, high lace-up boots, handbag hanging on her shoulder. She looked sixteen, maybe seventeen, could be younger. Sussock flashed his identification, 'Police,' he said.

'I'm just away home, sir.' The girl stepped off the steps with a flourish at her skirt and walked away quickly into the night.

'How far did you get?' Sussock stirred his coffee. He glanced out of the window and saw his reflection, thin drawn face, greying, and beyond his image, a crimson dawn was just beginning to break over the city.

'Not very far, I'm afraid.' Elka Willems sat opposite him, crisp white blouse, serge skirt; she cradled a mug of coffee on her lap. Already her mug was half empty and Sussock had noticed before how quickly she could drink hot tea or coffee, whereas he had always to let his cool. 'She appeared to have worked the street for all she was worth. According to her flatmate, she wanted to buy a house and settle down. Odd girl, the flatmate, if you ask me.'

'Oh?'

'Well, shocked at the news about Stephanie, smoked a lot to calm her down but quickly became detached. The deceased's room was locked so I couldn't get in, there ought to be a key in her possessions. She came from Bearsden but the flatmate didn't know of her home address. She's been lifted by Vice before but she apparently always gave her flat address. Can't blame her, it's permanent, and she wouldn't want her parents to know how she put bread on her table.'

'I'll check it anyway.' Sussock picked up the phone on his desk and dialled a two-figure internal number. 'Scottish Criminal Records Office? Yes, DS Sussock here, SCRO, P Division, can you send me the previous on one Stephanie Craigellachie, yes, Craigellachie, aged approximately twenty years, probably has an address in Gibson Street, Kelvinbridge. I'd be particularly interested in a previous address believed to be in Bearsden. Perhaps you could phone me back with any information and send the paperwork by courier at your earliest convenience. Thank you.' He replaced the receiver.

'So that's as far as I got,' said Elka Willems. 'She was earning money, taking home in a week, a good week, what I earn in three months. She was stashing it away somewhere, Building Society, I suppose.'

'Well, I'm afraid the p.m. didn't exactly bear that out.' Sussock drank his coffee, now cool enough for his taste. 'I'm afraid she was a smack head. All her money went on junk.'

'Oh.' Elka Willems was genuinely disappointed.

'She was a high risk AIDS carrier. She shot up, track

marks on both arms and in her neck. You didn't cut yourself when you were in her flat, no?'

'No.'

'Good. She also had an interesting tattoo.' He described the tattoo.

'So who is or who was Dino?'

'If we find that out we may be able to make great leaps forward,' said Sussock. 'But Dr Reynolds said that the tattoo wasn't new.' He glanced at his watch, 04.30 hours. 'You sign off in ninety minutes.'

'Yes,' she smiled, 'compensation of being of lowly rank: you tend to have a greater chance of getting off on time.'

'Don't remind me. I'll have to stay until I hand over to Fabian. I won't clear the station until nine-thirty a.m.'

'Coming round?'

He nodded. 'I'd like that.'

'I'll wait up.'

Sussock smiled. 'I'll call at the flat first, I think, see if there's any mail. I'm still waiting for the papers to come through. They could come any day now.'

'One day at a time, old Sussock, one day at a time.' She stood and collected both mugs and leant forward and kissed his forehead. He slipped an arm around her waist.

'Come on,' he said, 'you were the one who wanted to be discreet.'

'You're right.' She pulled herself away. 'Let's play pretend, Sergeant. I'll be off now. You've got a report to write.'

Sussock wrote up the report of the post mortem as neatly and fully as he could and, pending its being typed, folded it and placed it in Donoghue's pigeonhole. He checked his own pigeonhole. A circular about leave having to be taken within the calendar year, and not from April to April. He read it, digested it, screwed it into a ball and tossed it into a waste-paper basket. It was by then 06.30 hours. Tired cops were leaving the building. Fresh-faced ones were already in the muster room.

*

The man eased himself out of the bed and walked across the room, moving quietly and softly for such a large man. He opened the curtains, sunlight fell richly over the rooftops of Newton Mearns, and as it flooded out of the lace curtains he looked at suburbia, solid, expensive, prestigious housing, mature gardens, BMWs, Mercedes, Volvos in the drive-ways. He turned and looked at his wife, middle-aged like him, overweight like him, a lump in the yellow sheets. The central heating switched itself on and the trapped air bubble began to knock around the system, rattling in every room.

The central heating on, in mid-July, and a hot July at that, and those hideous yellow sheets.

The slumbering woman stirred, woken by the pipes knocking maybe, or by the sunlight streaming through the window, or by him moving and padding across the deep pile carpet.

Deep pile, had to be deep pile, and yellow. Had to be yellow too. More like a vast ochre sheepskin rug, he thought.

Soon she'd speak.

He didn't want her to speak. He didn't want to have to hear her voice, not yet, not just yet, her voice as though she was going to break into song any minute, but never did. Sing or talk, you big bitch, that's what he'd be thinking quite soon now, he knew he'd be thinking that. Sing or talk, as they dressed, as they breakfasted, passing the pieces of daintily cut toast, all without the crust, of course. He had tried to analyse her voice, it was pitched high to the back and top of her mouth, similar to the way he joined his mouth when he whistled. But she didn't whistle, she talked: a high-pitched wailing, plaintive, nearly a song: so plaintive.

It made him want to scream.

'Oh,' she said, 'you're up.'

'Yes, dear.' He turned to face her, leaning against the windowsill.

'Did you sleep, Dino?' she sang. 'Did you sleep well?'

CHAPTER 3

Wednesday 08.35–11.30 hours

Sussock sat in front of Donoghue's desk, silently waiting for Donoghue to read his report, handwritten. Donoghue had arrived at P Division at Charing Cross at 08.30 hours, was at his desk, 08.31 hours, first pipe of the day satisfactorily alight at 08.32 hours. After the pleasantries he spoke only one sentence to Ray Sussock. 'Can't make this out, this word here, Ray?'

Sussock leaned forward. 'Groin,' he said. 'She had a tattoo on her groin, sir.'

Donoghue grunted, took his pen and printed the word 'groin' over Sussock's illegible wriggle. 'Got to keep it legible for the girls in the typing pool, Ray.'

'Indeed, sir,' said the older man.

Donoghue read the reports, Sussock's report of the post mortem of Stephanie Craigellachie, and WPC Willems's account of her visit to the domicile of the deceased. Then, as Sussock had expected him to, Donoghue turned again to the front of both reports and he re-read them, digesting every detail; if he was eating a meal he would have been said to be masticating thoroughly.

Sussock shook the sleep from his eyes and tried to keep himself awake by focusing on the corner of the grey steel Scottish Office issue filing cabinet which stood behind and to one side of Donoghue's chair. Then he looked at Donoghue's desk top, the huge black ashtray big enough for one junior officer to have quipped in a moment of familiarity, 'All you need now is a couple of goldfish, sir,' the blotting-pad, fully redundant since the advent of the ballpoint pen but without which no desk looks complete. The telephone, the spread of reports and documents pleasingly untidy. Donoghue, Sussock had found, was a man of meticulous appearance and watch-setting punctuality, but his desk was often a human shifting sands of papers and files and memos. Sussock had long subscribed to the view that a tidy desk is the sign of a sick mind and despaired of the officers who had, it seemed to him, won promotion because at the end of their working day their desks were left clear and tidy, ruler just in front of the blotting-pad, three ballpoints in line abreast at the side, telephone in the right-hand corner, parallel with both edges of the desk. If he had realized that that was the secret years ago he might, he often thought, just might, have got somewhere. Instead he often left more papers on his desk than were in his filing cabinet, usually burying the telephone, and so at the age of fifty-five he had achieved the lofty rank of Detective-Sergeant and even then he felt his promotion had been in recognition of long service rather than merit. Hindsight, he often told himself is a wonderful thing, but he regretted not having realized the importance of a tidy desk, sick mind or no sick mind. Senior Officers, he felt, are not interested in what goes on in the street, they care only about what goes on in the building, tidy desks are important, neatly written, promptly delivered reports are important, as is a small knot in your tie, because a big knot is for woolly-minded liberals. All such things are more important than your arrest rate. That and drinking in the right pubs.

Sussock turned his gaze from Donoghue's desktop to the coat-stand adjacent to the filing cabinet on which Donoghue had hung his light-weight summer coat, a Burberry, and a cream-coloured hat in a near 'trilby' style. Pretty soon, after a few more minutes of meticulous digestion of points and information, Sussock knew that Donoghue would lean forward, laying down the reports on the blotting-pad and say, 'Right then, Ray, let's kick it about.' Sussock glanced to his right out of Donoghue's window and gazed up Sauchiehall

Street, angular buildings of stone and glass, buses with the liveries of half a dozen independent companies. His eyes swam and he shook his head again.

'All right, Ray.' Donoghue leaned forward and placed both reports side by side on the blotting-pad and took his pipe from his mouth. 'Let's kick it around a bit, shall we.' Sussock shuffled wearily in his chair.

'So she was murdered as we first suspected, the obvious wound was the only wound, hence the fatal one, she was murdered where she was found, she was a lady of the night and a heroin addict. Lived in a shared flat with a now shocked but none too sympathetic-sounding girlfriend. She was known to be frightened of a stockily built man who drives a decorated car and she has an interesting tattoo which indicates a present or past involvement with some-body called Dino. Is that a fair summary, Ray?'

'Yes, sir, also to include that she was murdered where she fell.'

'I think I said that. It's a valid point and means an appeal for witnesses.' Donoghue scribbled a note. 'Who's in today?'

'King and Montgomerie are both on day shift this week, sir. Abernethy's on the back shift for the week.'

'With yourself on the graveyard shift for your sins, Ray.' Donoghue smiled. 'Very well, I won't keep you any longer than necessary. The way I see it is that we have the following tasks; we need to search Stephanie Craigellachie's flat, find her home address in Bearsden because next of kin have still to be notified, talk to the girls in the street, that'll be for Abernethy to do. Anything else?'

'Find Dino?'

'Of course, Dino the mysterious,' said Donoghue, lighting his pipe with the gold-plated lighter, 'and find the identity of the owner of the fancy car. They may turn out to be one and the same.'

'They may indeed, sir.'

'See what rumours are flying around, if any. I'll ask

Montgomerie to pull his snout, Monday Morning or whatever his name is . . .'

'Tuesday Noon,' said Sussock. 'Montgomerie once
told me his real name but I can't recall it. He was born
one Tuesday at noon and the name has stuck since childhood.'

'Tuesday Noon,' said Donoghue. 'Still, he's been useful
before, no matter what his name is.'

'All we're waiting for is feedback from Forensic and the
knife and the clothing.'

'Where's the girl's handbag?'

'Stores.'

'I see. I think that'll be King's first job while Montgomerie's contacting Tuesday Noon'.

'Will that be all, sir?'

'Yes, thank you, Ray. See you at the hand-over tomorrow
morning.'

'Good day, sir.' Sussock stood and Donoghue noticed
how tired and drawn he looked, how elderly. He was too
old to be at the front line of police work.

'Have a good sleep, Ray,' he said.

'Don't you usually have female officers with you when you
go into a woman's room?' The girl hung back leaning against
the wall of the kitchen, interested and uninterested at the
same time. Detached, thought King, a very detached young
woman. Not a healthy state of mind.

'Not if there isn't a lady involved,' he said, 'as is the case
here.' He pressed his shoulder to the door of Stephanie
Craigellachie's room. The barrel lock sagged into wet-rotten
wood. 'Sure you don't have a key?'

'Sure I'm sure,' said the girl, Karen by name.

'It'll break cleanly,' said Montgomerie. King shoved it
and it broke cleanly.

Stephanie Craigellachie's room was small, cramped,
spare and spartan. A single bed, two ruffled sheets and a

blanket, insufficient for winter, but this was high summer, right enough; no pillow, a chest of drawers, bare floorboards, save for a rug, torn curtains, dirty windows. A wardrobe without a door revealed her clothing, a few dresses, skirts, a woollen pullover rolled up on the top shelf, a winter coat, torn at the elbow.

Something on legs scuttled across the floor and into a hole in the corner of the room.

'Ugh!' said Karen, craning her neck around the corner of the doorway. 'I've never seen in here before. She never let me in, wonder what she did with her money, stashed it away, I reckon, got to be a Building Society passbook somewhere if we look for it. Saving for a flat in the south side, must have wanted it so bad to be prepared to live like this, I mean not spending on herself. You want me to make a start in the chest of drawers?'

'No. We want you to remain in the kitchen,' said Montgomerie harshly. 'Just keep out of the room.'

'Oh!' Karen said with unashamed disappointment. But she didn't argue. 'Wonder why she didn't spend on herself? I mean, a little luxury helps the world go round.'

'She spent on herself all right,' said Montgomerie, moving past King and opening the dirty curtains a little, just enough to look down into Gibson Street. An Asian family, baggy trousers and saris ambling gauchely up the road, a lemon-haired girl in a long skirt and blouse swaying confidently in the opposite direction, the basement restaurants, the second-hand bookshops, the antique shops, the bridge, the trees in the park, the graceful curve of the Elden Street tenement block, empty now, awaiting a decision as to its fate. A red fly poster said, 'Save Elden Street.'

'What do you mean?' Karen looked at Montgomerie. 'She must have been pulling down hundreds of pounds a week. What did she do with it, where did she put it?'

King opened the top drawer of the chest of drawers and took out a hypodermic syringe, broken and rusty.

'Handle with care,' said Montgomerie, 'she's a category one risk.'

'Of what?' said Karen.

'AIDS,' said King, placing the dirty works on top of the chest of drawers. 'She was a smack head.'

'I never knew . . .'

'Maybe you just didn't want to know,' said King. 'Girl works the street seven nights a week, nothing to show for it.'

'She did as well,' said Karen, 'seven nights each week every week. Never missed a shift, winter or summer.'

'A shift.'

'Just an expression.' Karen went back to the kitchen and sat at the table. She wore a black T-shirt, short black skirt and black tights, and King noticed how thin her legs were, anorexically thin. Perhaps she was clinically depressed, he thought, perhaps that's why she seems so detached.

'Only one thing drives a girl to do that, Karen,' said King from Stephanie Craigellachie's room, 'and it's not the dream of a bought three apartment in the south side.'

'I know,' said Karen.

'She was spending it all on junk.' King opened the other drawers as Montgomerie sifted through clothes hanging in the wardrobe.

'She was a really nice girl,' said Karen. 'Brought a cat home once, found it in the gutter, leg smashed, then she took it to the Dispensary for Sick Animals, walked all the way. She was that sort of girl. Just kept telling me she was saving for a flat.'

'Ever seen her arms?' asked King.

'Her arms?' Karen shook her head. 'She liked long-sleeved blouses and dresses. Even in the summer.'

'Ever think she might be covering herself up?'

'No.' The girl's expression became vacant, as if the real world was catching her through her detachment.

'Been on the street yourself, then?' asked Montgomerie gently.

'No. Yes. Sometimes. Just when I needed money.' She looked at Montgomerie appreciatively. He was tall, flat stomach, chiselled features, downturned moustache.

'Do you see it as a way of life?'

She cast a feminine eye over King. Chubby, bearded, sort of homely, a family man, she thought, whereas the tall thin one would be playing the field for all he was worth. She shrugged in reply to the question.

'Just do some growing up first,' said King without looking at her.

'You're not really ready for the street.' Montgomerie took a dress from where it hung in the wardrobe, looked at it, then laid it on the bed. 'Nobody ever is, but you're a little more vulnerable than most. Nobody ever offered you anything to make you feel good?'

'Not yet.'

'Not yet is the right answer. There's always somebody to help you out if you go on to the streets.'

'I wouldn't take anything from a strange man.'

Montgomerie groaned with disappointment. She even sounded like a little girl. 'It's not strange men who'd give you anything. It's men you've known a long time, or other women that you think are your mates. They'll offer you a little packet of angel dust: a short step to the good life.' He extended his arm to indicate Stephanie Craigellachie's room. 'Take a look at the good life.'

'Hey, I don't need a sermon.'

'So tell us a little more about Stephanie,' said Montgomerie. 'I mean, now you know that she was a smack head.'

'I don't know nothing more. I told the female cop everything I know.'

'Come on, Karen!'

She shot a glance at Montgomerie, stung by his anger,

alarmed by his impatience. 'Well, she didn't have any friends, didn't seem to have anyway, came from Bearsden, she was already in here when I took the second room.'

'Ever mention anybody called Dino?'

'Dino?' She copied Montgomerie's pronunciation, 'Die-no.'

'Dino.'

She shook her head.

'Sure?'

'Nobody of that name. Did mention a Dino from time to time.' She said 'Dee-no'.

'Dino,' echoed Montgomerie.

King in the cramped smack-head cell turned to Karen, interestedly. 'What did she say about him?'

'Not a lot.'

'Not much to tell us then, is there.' Montgomerie took out his notebook.

Karen lit a nail, inhaled deeply and exhaled down her nose.

'Don't keep us waiting.' Montgomerie sat at the table opposite the girl.

'Last person to sit in that chair was Stephanie Craigellachie,' said Karen comfortingly.

'Then it's a good job I'm not superstitious,' Montgomerie replied coldly, impatiently. 'So, Dino?'

'Dino.' Karen inhaled again. This time the smoke came out of her mouth as she spoke. 'She mentioned him a lot; no, she didn't. What I mean is she thought a lot of him, liked him. Didn't say much about him but when she did talk about him you could tell she liked him, by the way she talked.'

'I see.' Montgomerie still hadn't written a word in his notebook. 'Any idea of his identity?'

She shook her head. 'He was just a guy.'

'You can do better than that.'

'Well, I got the impression that he had a bit of money. I

mind the times she used to come back early, said she'd met
Dino, he'd taken her for a meal and had given her enough
cash to keep her off the street for the rest of the night. Look,
you maybe ought to talk to the girls who work the street,
they'd know more than me.'

'Apparently so,' said Montgomerie, 'if you lived with her
for a matter of months and still didn't know she was a dope
fiend. Not a lot gets noticed by you, aye? So how often did
she meet Dino?'

'Once a fortnight, once every ten days, once a week. No
set pattern.'

'You said she had no other friends?'

Karen shook her head. 'None that I knew of, or know of.
She went out, came in, stayed in until she went out again.
It all figures now. See, the way she talked about that three
apartment south of the water. Sort of lived for it but never
got nearer to it, like a gold prospector chewing dirt for
twenty years and just living for the day he strikes it rich,
but never does so, yet he keeps going anyway. Must have
been like a dream. I reckon we all need a dream to cling on
to, something to work towards. For Stephanie it was a three
apartment in the south side. Didn't really want much, did
she, no.'

'Where did Stephanie come from? Bearsden is a big place.'

'She didn't talk much about her background. Just
Bearsden where even the muggers say "please". Couldn't
be more different from my background. I come from Airdrie.
Things are so bad there they take the pavements in at night.'

King and Montgomerie split up. King returned to P
Division and consulted the yellow pages, making a note of
the city's tattoo artists. Montgomerie went to St George's,
one stop by tube from Kelvinbridge, and walked up towards
the Round Toll. He went into a bar called the Gay Gordon.
He was looking for a guy called Tuesday Noon.

The Gay Gordon was a tough, rough pub, it was a

concrete pillbox of a bar on the corner of a piece of waste
ground; opposite, on the other side of the road, was a spread
of new factory units; behind them on a hillside was a
concrete and glass complex of a huge housing scheme,
looking not unlike a modern prison. Montgomerie entered
the Gay Gordon via the narrow metal doors. It was still just
11.30 a.m., the pub had been open for business for thirty
minutes and would remain open for the next eleven and a
half hours selling cheap wines and spirits, plenty of choice
of either but only one tap of lager. There was just one room
in the Gay Gordon, hard chairs and tables chained to the
floor as much to stop the punters taking them to furnish
their homes as it was to stop them being used as weapons
in the inevitable Friday night rammy. Along the wall opposite the gantry was a red upholstered bench, badly
slashed, with the stuffing pulled out in dull white plumes.
The barman was a hard-looking, bald-headed guy who gave
Montgomerie a mean look as he entered, a look which said
very clearly that cops and sawdust don't mix. Not in the
Gay Gordon. Above the gantry was a television mounted
on the wall with both the colour and the volume turned up
too loudly. At the moment it was horse-racing being beamed
from a shire county in England. It might as well have been
beamed into the Gay Gordon from another planet. Two
young guys in Oxfam cast-offs slumped together in the far
corner staring blankly into space, smashed on cheap junk.
Tuesday Noon was sitting on the bench nearer to the door,
underneath a window through which streamed a beam of
sunlight which illuminated the flecks of dust floating in the
air inside the bar. Montgomerie went up to the gantry and
ordered a lager and a whisky. The barman looked at him
coldly and then served him slowly in his own good time.
Montgomerie picked up the drinks and walked across the
tacky lino and sat opposite Tuesday Noon, pulling the chair
from the table as far as the silver chain would allow.

    'Hi, ya, Tuesday.' Montgomerie put the whisky down on

the table in front of Tuesday Noon, who picked up the glass and sank the contents in one, neat. He rasped a hot breath of thanks across the tabletop. He had a black mouth with a few bent yellow pegs going up and down. He pushed the empty glass across the table towards Montgomerie.

'Not so fast off your mark, Tuesday,' said Montgomerie. 'I want a wee chat first.'

'Aye?' Tuesday Noon's hot breath blasted across the table.

'You heard about the lassie who was filled in just off Blythswood Square last night?'

'Aye. I read about it in the *Record*.'

'That's what I'm interested in.'

'Aye?' He wasn't giving anything away.

Montgomerie suddenly wondered how old Tuesday Noon was, he could be as young as forty or as old as sixty, grey whiskers, grimy face, matted hair, same old scarf round his neck winter and summer. 'Heard anything?'

'Not yet.'

Quite clever, Tuesday, quite clever.

'Been up the Square recently?'

'Not really my part of town, Mr Montgomerie.' He pushed the empty glass further across the table towards Montgomerie.

'We're interested in a character called Dino. Ring any bells, no?'

Tuesday Noon shook his head. 'Never heard nothing about no Dino.'

'Not worth another drink then, is it.' Montgomerie drank his lager in three deep draughts.

'Did hear of something else.'

'Oh?'

'Yes.'

'Information first, Tuesday, drink later, if it's worth it.'

'Heard of the Black Team?'

Montgomerie shook his head.

'Come on, Tuesday, I'm not a fish on the end of a line.
Stop playing games or you get bounced into the cells.'

'For what?'

'All those unpaid fines. Have you any idea of the amount
of outstanding warrants out on you? You can get pulled any
time we please. Just happens that you're more useful to us
on the streets, but that's not a guarantee of liberty so don't
abuse the privilege or you get taken to your wee home from
home.'

'OK, OK. The Black Team, women, all women, too old
to work the street any more, they jump young girls at the
end of the night, roll them for their night's takings.'

'At the end of the night?'

'Towards the end of it. There's not a lot of point doing it
in the early evening, the purses are still empty then, also
it's still light. They have to wait till dark, have to wait till
the girls have taken a good few quid, turned a few tricks. If
they roll five girls they pick up a good few hundred quid for
twenty minutes' work. Sometimes they don't have to roll
them, just walk up to them and show them the knife . . .'

'I see.'

'Or threaten to give them a doing. Any sensible girl will
give up her wedge, she can work an extra hour or so and
make up the loss. So she's late to her bed but at least she
lives and can still work. You know what women can be like
to each other, and where one old woman can stick a younger
one with a knife or chair leg to make sure she doesn't work
again for weeks, if at all.'

'The Black Team?'

'That's it, Mr Montgomerie.'

'I just can't see a team of women rolling down the hill
knocking over all the girls. The girls would stand there
waiting for it.'

'The girls kept getting picked up and dropped off all the
time. A girl gets brought back to the street by a trick, gets
out of the motor and next minute, before she knows where

she is, the Black Team have got her against the wall. I'd say that was worth a drink, Mr Montgomerie.'

Montgomerie grunted and twisted himself out of his seat and walked up to the gantry. He brought a whisky back and handed it to Tuesday Noon. The glass didn't touch the table. Tuesday Noon threw the wee goldie back in one and then sat back cradling the glass with a gleam of satisfaction in his eyes.

'Keep your ears to the ground, Tuesday.' Montgomerie remained standing. 'It was a nasty attack, just last night, stabbed in the throat, girl in her early twenties, frightened of a guy who drives a tarted-up car and knew somebody called Dino.'

'Dino?'

'Dino. She was also a smack head.'

'Drug scene is too tight for me to get near, you know that, Mr Montgomerie.'

'I know that, but you know the users, the guys and chicks at the bottom end of the ladder. See if they knew this girl, Stephanie Craigellachie, see if they know of a Dino, maybe there's a pusher called Dino, see if they know of a guy who drives a flash motor. Just ask around, Tuesday, keep sniffing. You know all the rat holes in this town, so go to work. You know the number to call when you've got gold dust to trade.'

Ray Sussock had driven home. Home, his 'temporary accommodation' as he called it, although he began to feel a nagging fear, something that he couldn't easily define or recognize, but a feeling akin to despair as he realized that 'temporariness' had succeeded in dragging itself from deep mid-winter well into summer. Autumn was on the horizon and with it the prospect of over-wintering in the present accommodation until the arrival of the property buoyancy which came with each spring. He pulled his car up to the kerb and got out of the vehicle feeling tired, heavy-eyed, grimy, not at all able to enjoy the fresh July morning. He let himself into the large house, once the immense home of a wealthy family, now broken up into a warren of bedsitters run by a Polish landlord, resident of the basement flat. He checked the table in the hall, plenty of mail, but none for him. Nothing unusual in that. The house was at that moment quiet, those residents who worked would be long gone, those who didn't work would be still in bed. What's the point in getting up if there's nothing to get up for, fresh July morning or not?

Sussock went into the kitchen he shared with three other flats. A small kitchenette, a gas cooker, some shelves, a fridge. Below the kitchen, down a turning stair, was the landlord's flat. Sussock had been there once, he went there to ask for a light bulb, he had been refused, been told coldly and briskly by the small man to get his own. He was surprised by the landlord's accommodation, having always assumed that the massive sum of rents generated by the old house must have gone towards the upkeep of a lavishly decorated flat, but in the event the thin gaunt landlord and his enormous cold-eyed wife, both of whom never failed to remind Sussock of Jack Spratt and spouse, lived in an icy cramped kitchen, where they sat during the day and the evening with their television perched on the sink unit and beyond that was their bedroom with a bed and a wardrobe and nothing else. Following the eye-opening surprise of their standard of living Sussock liked them no more but he did find a sense of respect for them growing, in that they lived in spartan accommodation and expected their tenants to do the same. After that it was easier for him to accept his own dingy 'temporary accommodation'.

That morning, in the kitchen, he found that someone had pilfered his last remaining tea-bag: low trick, that, even for the bedsits. He also discovered that his shelf in the fridge had been raided and that someone with a missing top incisor, he noted with a professional eye, had taken a bite out of his Scottish Cheddar. So he raided someone else's coffee. It was by such means, he had learned, that one survives in bed sit land.

He carried the steaming mug of coffee upstairs continuing to enjoy the silence of the house. The orginal large rooms had been divided by wretchedly thin room dividers and sound polluted badly from flat to flat. He entered his own room and sat in the armchair and kicked his shoes off and toyed with the idea of grabbing the golden opportunity to sleep before the couple upstairs commenced their daily screaming sessions. They were a couple who clearly, to Sussock, had a relationship which thrived on conflict and which would probably escalate and escalate until one knifed the other and the knifer would then sit sobbing over the corpse of the knifed protesting love of the purest and undying kind. Sussock was also acutely aware that soon the boys in the next room would be very likely to begin their morning coupling, the grunts of which were even more distasteful a sound to have to sit and listen to than the gasps and sighs of the sexual activity of the more mainstream kind which came through the other wall of his room. It was also quiet from directly above but only until the young office worker came home and stamped across his floor, Sussock's ceiling, and switched on his hi-fi, and sent the base notes boom, boom, booming downward into Sussock's flat.

But at that moment it was quiet. The birds sang out-side; they made the only sound. It was tempting. The bed in the corner looked tempting and he was tired. She'd understand, even though he'd said that he'd see her later in the morning she knew fine well that if he wasn't round by 11.00 he wouldn't be coming until much later, after a kip, after a few 'zs'. He could phone but that would involve having to go down to Byres Road and if he was going out at all he might as well drive over to Langside. He unbuttoned his cuffs and tugged off his tie. No contest, really.

*

'Got to be a scratcher, Jim,' said the man, well built, stocky, dark hair. Serious hard eyes.

'A scratcher?' said King.

'What we call "scratchers" in the trade, bungling cow-boys, get them everywhere.' The man studied the photograph. 'Aye, we get them everywhere, prisons, backyards, dodgy studios. You want AIDS or Hepatitis B, go to a scratcher. See me, I use clean needles, clean tubes, clean tubs, fresh ink and fresh pair of surgical gloves with each client and that's why I cost. I also test for pigmentation allergy.'

'Pigmentation allergy?'

The man shrugged. 'Pigmentation allergy. Some people are allergic to tattoo artists' ink, usually the colour red for a reason I don't understand, but it's almost always red which brings them out in a rash so severe that they want to sit up at night trying to scratch the tattoo off. But see me, I test for it. It's a simple five-minute test, but I do it for each patient, that's why I cost too. I do the test for each and every client.'

The man glanced at the photograph again. He stood at the entrance to his studio. A client, a customer, a man in his early thirties with a pencil line moustache sat patiently in the chair which reclined like a dentist's chair. Tubs of various coloured inks stood on the table beside the chair, in front of him was the tattooist's chair, vacant, and beside which the tattooist's instruments were arranged in a rack, all shiny and chrome. The walls of the studio were covered in an impressive collage of examples of the tattoos available.

King had entered the studio, first a waiting-room just off a side street off Duke Street. The walls of the waiting-room were covered in a similar collage of tattoos to those which decorated the surgery, the rooms being separated by a pane of glass. Two young women sat in the waiting-room, or rather they sat on the hard bench which ran round the walls of the room. King pondered on the design and location of their tattoos. A man sat in the corner of the room patiently leafing through a magazine. The girls glanced at each other and giggled. Their first visits, thought King, though the man seems quite at home and was perhaps calling to have another design added to what might already be an impressive piece of body art. There were notices on the wall, refreshingly breaking up the collage. 'Ass or Arse, Bum or Buttock, we don't tattoo, nor stomachs, nor genitalia. We just don't, so don't ask.' Another poster showed a young man with a dotted line tattooed round his neck, under which the words 'cut here' had been tattooed. The caption read: 'Nothing stupid done, what may be funny at eighteen when you're drunk is not so funny twenty-four hours later, still less twenty-four years later. So don't ask.' Another poster showed modification work, how clumsy amateurish tattoos could be transferred into more presentable examples of the art.

King had stood at the entrance to the studio. The tattooist had glanced at him and then returned his concentration to his customer's arm and seemed to King to be alternating the needle between a series of fine sharp pecking movements, and a series of gentle down strokes. There was no smell. That had surprised King. He had expected the studio of a tattooist to smell, he didn't know what of, but he had expected a smell of some kind but there was nothing, no sweat, no disinfectant smell, no ink odour, nothing. Arid. Again the tattooist had looked at King.

'Can't you read, Jim?' he said.

King looked to one side and read. The sign said: 'If you've got nothing to do, don't do it here.'

'Police,' said King and flashed his identification.

The tattooist seemed to growl and then added a few more downward strokes to his customer's arm and having timed King's patience span to a millisecond, managed to put the needle down just before King was going to suggest that he might like to shut down for the rest of the day and have a cosy chat at the police station.

'Yes?' The man walked across the studio floor to where King stood at the doorway.

King showed him a photograph of Stephanie Craigellachie's tattoo.

'Oh,' said the man, not shaken, not surprised.

'Recognize the work?'

The man shook his head. He pointed to the sign which made reference to buttocks, stomachs and genitalia.

'I don't know whether you'd call this genitalia or not,' he said, 'but it's close enough for me to back off. I wouldn't do anything like it. That goes for every reputable artist that I know. Has to be the work of a scratcher.'

'A scratcher?'

'What we call scratchers in the trade, bungling cowboys, get them everywhere, prisons, backyards, dodgy studios . . .'

King was impressed that the man seemed to be genuinely looking at the tattoo and not a close-up photograph of the sort that could easily circulate in grimy bars.

'See—' he ran his hand along the photograph of the tattoo—'it's blurred, soft at the edges, poor spacing, it's the sort of thing that school kids do to each other with pins.'

'Pins?'

'Take one ordinary pin, a ball of cotton wool, ordinary ink, soak a small wad of cotton wool in the ink, wrap it round the point of the pin and tap the needle into the skin. The pin pricks the skin and the ink runs off the cotton wool and remains under the skin. It's a simple and crude tattoo, works as well in that it doesn't wash off, and doesn't distort too much over time.'

'So we're looking for a scratcher?'

'If you're looking for the man or woman who did that, then yes, you're looking for a scratcher.'

'Tell me,' said King, recovering the photograph, 'how long would a tattoo like that take to apply?'

'Two hours, three at the outside.'

'As long as that?'

'Yes,' said the man, glancing wonderingly at the two young females who continued to glance at each other and giggle. 'It's a rough piece of work, I can't see sign of any sophisticated instrument being used if any instrument was used at all. Tell you something else: it would have been painful for the girl.'

'It would?'

'Aye. Doesn't take much imagination to think of the discomfort of a few thousand pin jabs in that part of your body. I'd say it was done over two or three or four sittings. It wouldn't have been comfortable. Tattooing isn't comfortable. It's not uncomfortable if it's done properly, but it's not comfortable either. This would have been very uncomfortable.'

'Could it be self-inflicted?'

The man shook his head. 'Can't see it,' he said. 'It's possible in that you can reach that part of your body quite easily, but it would be too prolonged and painful to be a self-tattoo. "I belong to Dino." It's more like she lay back, bit the bullet, thought long and hard of Scotland and let somebody, maybe Dino, go to work on her.'

'You don't know of a scratcher called Dino by any chance?'

The man didn't. Said he had a customer waiting if that was all.

Did he know of any scratchers, period?

Anyone with a pin and wad of cotton wool is a scratcher, period.

'There's one, though, just off London Road, got a sign in the window of his house, "Tattoos done". I only heard about him. I don't know him. It's the only one I've heard of. They tend to be underground.'

King said, 'Thanks.'

CHAPTER 4

Wednesday, 11.30–15.30 hours

Donoghue sifted the items found in Stephanie Craigellachie's handbag. All had been dusted for prints and all had
revealed nothing but the prints of the dead girl, 'spur on
whorl of right aspect of right thumb,' read Bothwell's report.
The items had all been exposed to the meticulous attention
of Dr Jean Kay of the Forensic Science Laboratory at Pitt
Street along with the dead girl's clothing. Dr Kay's report
and findings lay at the side of Donoghue's desk. The handbag and items it contained had been 'processed' and he
could handle them as he wished, yet for some reason he
held the handbag as though it might crumble to his touch
and he sifted the items by moving them on his desktop with
the tip of his ballpoint.

The bag was of cheap patent leather, torn here and there,
with a long strap enabling it to be worn at the shoulder.
Donoghue had hoped that the tacky smooth surface of the
bag might have revealed interesting fingerprints, hopefully
of her attacker who might have tried to snatch the bag from
her. But as in the case of the items the bag contained, the
only latents to be lifted were those belonging to the deceased
whose next of kin, he reminded himself, had still to be
informed and who had still to make a formal identification
of the body. It was an important step because Donoghue
knew fine well that the real Stephanie Craigellachie could
be alive and well and living in happy retirement in Partick,
and she could be known to the deceased girl in some capacity
who was using her name as a *nom de rue*. It was a possibility
but, he conceded, not by any means a likely one. His 'inner
voice', as he called it, and to which he had long learned to

listen, told him that he was dealing with the murder of Stephanie Craigellachie and with no other, that the handbag belonged to Stephanie Craigellachie and no other, and that the contents summed up the empty, bleak, desperate existence that had been the life of Stephanie Craigellachie and the life of no other.

He sifted the items, continuing to use his ballpoint pen to do so. There was the purse, cheap, red, a subway ticket, some loose change, he counted seventy-three pence. And therein lay the first mystery. She had been murdered at approximately 22.30 hours and was known to be on the streets from approximately 17.00 hours each night. She was doing good business, there ought to have been a wedge in the handbag, a substantial wad, rolled tight and held with a rubber band perhaps, not just a lousy seventy-three pence.

So, he thought, it would be not unreasonable to assume that the motive for the murder was robbery. It was, he told himself, an assumption, to bear in mind, to keep in play, but not to the exclusion of other motives because it was a dangerously inviting conclusion to leap towards.

He took his pipe from the ashtray and lit it with his lighter and leaned back in his chair. He glanced out of his window at the funnel that was Sauchiehall Street, concrete and glass buildings mixed with old stonework, the sun played on the glass and the car windscreens, buses stood bumper to bumper. He glanced up into the blue, near-cloudless sky and wondered why it was that he was not prepared to accept readily that the murder of Stephanie Craigellachie was a question of a mugging which went too far.

If, he pondered, a man was going to rob a girl like Stephanie, then surely he would do it by enticing her into his car, drive her some place quiet, produce a knife and say 'pay and get out'. He would not attack her in Blythswood Street where there is a lot of traffic, both vehicular and pedestrian, there would be girls to come and help out, cops patrolling, men looking for business who hopefully would not stand by to see a girl rolled for her wad. Yet he attacked her in the street. If, of course, it was a man.

Point two—Donoghue's eye was caught by a gull swooping and soaring over Strathclyde House—point two, if the attacker hadn't got a car into which he or she could entice her, how did he make her retreat into the alley? If the attacker's approach was threatening, then she would have stepped into the brighter lights of Blythswood Square or St Vincent Street at the intersection of Blythswood Street. Yet it seemed she was forced to run into the alley.

Or was she enticed into the alley?

Donoghue sucked and blew his pipe. Blue smoke hung in layers in his room. It was clear in Dr Reynolds's report that Stephanie Craigellachie was stabbed where she was found, one blow, or thrust, immediately fatal, and she slumped to the ground. So she entered the alley either to meet someone whom she trusted or to escape someone she feared. Someone perhaps who knew where to find her?

So where was all her money? Had she given it all willingly to the person who enticed her into the alley? Did the person who stabbed her snatch the money to make the murder look like a cheap and grubby 'accident', whereas the real intention was to snuff out her life all along for a motive yet to be determined?

Or—and Donoghue began to warm to this notion—did she see someone, someone she recognized, turn into Blythswood Street, someone in a black car perhaps, turn down the one-way street from the Square, and she hoped to avoid him by darting into the alley before he saw her, and had thrown her wad away before he caught her, if he caught her? But caught her he evidently and eventually had. Donoghue tried to recall what was on either side of the alley, high walls and the back of buildings on one side, on the other, a wooden fence and then a building site where the façade of a Victorian building was being retained but the interior being demolished for complete rebuilding. It would have been very easy for her to reach into her bag and toss her money over the fence as she ran into the alley, hoping perhaps to recover it at a later stage.

Donoghue reached forward, grabbed the phone and dialled a two-figure internal number.

'Montgomerie,' replied a crisp, clipped voice.

'DI Donoghue.'

'Yes, sir.'

'What have you got on at the moment?'

'Writing up, sir,' replied Montgomerie. 'Visit to the deceased's flat, interview with her flatmate, contact with my snout.'

'Come up with anything?'

'Not a lot, sir.' Montgomerie cleared his throat. 'Most interesting information is a reference to a squad called the Black Team. I've never heard of them before, but they appear to be a group of retired ladies who prey on the working girls, those still young enough to work, the teenagers and those in their early twenties. By "retired" I mean over thirty. Could be a lead.'

'Could indeed.' Donoghue laid his pipe down. 'Could indeed. I'd like you to contact the uniform branch, please, and organize a sweep of the building site next to the alley, paying particular attention to the area close to the wooden fence. It occurred to me that she may have tossed her money over the fence before she was murdered. If she tossed her money she may also have thrown something else which could be of use to us.'

'Very good, sir. I'll get right on it.'

Donoghue replaced the telephone receiver. He thought about the Black Team. Yes, could indeed be interesting.

He returned his attention to the contents of Stephanie Craigellachie's handbag. A packet of tissues: he took each separate tissue from the wrapper and examined it, nothing hidden in the packet among the tissues. Half a dozen heavy duty condoms, a comb with a spiked handle, a spray of hair lacquer, both defensive weapons, essential equipment for a working girl, a packet of cigarettes, medium tar, and again nothing in the packet beside the nails. A cigarette lighter, plastic, disposable, marked 'Corfu'. Nothing else, nothing certainly as interesting as an address book with an entry under D for Dino.

He picked up Dr Kay's report on the forensic tests conducted on the clothing of the deceased. It did not surprise him that she noted the underclothing to be heavily stained with semen and 'female discharge'. Dr Kay could say little about the clothing other than that it was old, inexpensive and unclean.

The murder weapon also lay on Donoghue's desk, carefully wrapped in Cellophane and neatly labelled. It was an ordinary five-inch-bladed wooden-handled kitchen knife, every home has one, and it is largely because of that that it is also Scotland's number one murder weapon. It easily comes to hand during domestic disputes, which for some reason most often occur in the kitchen of a home, and such a knife is easily concealed in the jeans pocket of the sixteen-year-old son of the householder: he picks it up, goes out for the evening and gets into a fight. Elliot Bothwell had not been able to lift any latents whatsoever from the blade or the handle and could only regretfully conclude in his report that the killer wore gloves during the attack. Dr Kay in her report could only confirm that the blood on the blade and handle coincided with the blood group of the deceased as provided in information contained in the post mortem report.

Not a great deal to go on. Donoghue took his pipe from his mouth and scraped the waste ash into the ashtray. Just a dead heroin addict in a city of three million people, one fatal blow to her throat which could have been accidental, which in turn meant that the killer might never be traced if it was nothing more than an opportunist attack, one very curious tattoo naming a man or a woman called Dino who might or might not be implicated. No money on the girl's person. It was just a cheap, senseless mugging, Donoghue kept coming back to that possibility and just as quickly kept veering away again. No, she couldn't have run into the alley to escape a mugger or the Black Team. He thought that he would like to know a little more about the Black Team, he'd like to know more about the man in the black car who seemed to have terrified Stephanie Craigellachie herself, the scarlet woman who like so many people in his professional life was already, as the ambulance crews would code it, 'condition purple' by the time he first heard their name or knew they existed. Had existed.

'Aren't you taking the dog a walk today, Dino, you always do when you work at home? You said you'd work in the study, you know you said you'd work in the study because you mess up the living-room with your files, and have you paid the paper bill for last week, you know Mr Lennie is always too polite to ask and things must be tight for him in that little shop?'

'Yes, dear,' said Dino and took Sam to the grounds of the Burrell Collection and let him romp while he sat on the grass and watched the coachloads of trippers come and go. Then the springer spaniel nuzzled up close to him.

Suddenly the dog seemed the only substantial thing in his life. He said, 'Where is she, Sam? Where has she gone?'

The sunlight woke Sussock, streaming in through the thin faded curtains. He awoke slowly. It still felt unnatural to wake in the afternoon. Even now after a working life governed by shifts he had never, and doubted that he ever would, get used to going to bed and waking up again on the same day. He drew the palms of his hands down over his lean hungry face and realized that at the age of fifty-five the normal pattern of life wherein one wakes with each new day had been something he had not largely shared in. Waking

each day in the morning would be the novelty in his retirement, the compensation for just one more privation of being
a cop. He glanced at his watch: 03.05 p.m.

Six hours' sleep. Not bad. He could cope with six hours'
sleep. It gave him seven hours before signing on again for
the graveyard shift at 10.00 p.m.

He rolled out of bed and pulled on a pair of trousers. As
he did so he became aware of music penetrating the wall,
not loudly, but penetrating just the same. It came from the
left-hand wall, from the room occupied by the two boys who
wore their jerseys tucked into their trousers and who might
be seen walking late at night in Kelvinway, just strolling,
and approaching cars which pulled up alongside them.
Occasionally seen walking in our out of the gloom of the
parkland at either side of the Kelvinway.

Sussock wondered if their music had woken him and not
the sunlight. As he did so he felt a sudden flood of anger that
his personal space had been invaded. But the music was low,
it was as low as could reasonably be expected. It was the
paper thin walls that let in the sound, not the boys' anti-social
behaviour, and he had had six hours' sleep. The sun *was*
streaming in, he had always been light-sensitive, finding it
easy to rise in the summer and next to impossible in the winter.
So, he told himself, it was the sun that woke him.

He switched on his radio to drown out the boys' music
and to control his own personal space. He left his room and
went along to the bathroom he shared with three other flats.
He found that somebody had shaved and had left their
whiskers all over the wash-hand basin.

Montgomerie stood next to the sergeant of the uniformed
branch. The site foreman stood next to the sergeant. They
watched a line of constables in white short-sleeved shirts
pick their way over the rubble.

'What are you doing here?' Montgomerie looked across
the broad chest of the sergeant towards the site foreman.

'Gutting,' said the foreman. He wore a yellow hard hat, was stripped to the waist with a huge beer belly flopping over the belt of his jeans. 'We have to retain the frontage.' He nodded behind him and the wall which loomed above them. 'Got to retain the front of the building, the Victorian line, but we can do what we like behind. It'll be a bonny building when we're done, sell it nay bother, nay bother at all, all the benefits of modern building technology inside and all the grace of an old architectural design at the front, not just slabs of concrete and sheets of glass but real masonry.'

Montgomerie glanced behind him at the crew who sat on piles of rubble and leaned on picks, watching the searching cops.

The foreman followed Montgomerie's gaze. 'No reason why they shouldn't continue working,' he said wryly, 'but they won't, any excuse will do. I know, I used to be one of them, but you get promotion and see how your attitude changes.'

The line of cops worked up by the yellow fence. Occasionally a cop would stoop, pick something up, examine it and then toss it away. Then one cop in the middle of the line seemed to Montgomerie to snatch at something on the ground. He glanced at it quickly and left the line, stepping nimbly across the site and approached Montgomerie. 'Found this, sir.'

He handed Montgomerie a wallet.

'Found on the site, sir,' said Montgomerie.

Donoghue turned the wallet over in his hands.

'The squad is still on the site, sir,' said Montgomerie as an afterthought. 'But I think that may be what we're looking for.'

'It looks like it,' said Donoghue, slowly emptying the contents of the wallet on to his desktop. 'Take a seat, please.'

Montgomerie sat. He was not, he knew, wholly in the

Detective-Inspector's favour and being asked to sit instead of being kept standing was an unusual and valued sign of approval.

'Have you looked at the contents, Montgomerie?'

Montgomerie shook his head. 'No, sir, brought it straight as soon as I saw the name Stephanie Craigellachie inside.'

'Good man,' Donoghue examined the wallet's contents. Nearly £200.00 in cash, a Cellophane packet, creased and worn and containing isolated grains of yellow powder which Donoghue assumed to be the remnants of a sizeable and valuable bulk of heroin, a letter to Stephanie Craigellachie with a printed address on the top right hand corner, an address in Stirling Way, Bearsden. He read it. It was a short, somewhat sour note, he thought, advising Stephanie that 'Father' had been in hospital, not serious, just observation, out now, 'doubt if you'd be interested anyway, but I'm telling you just the same'. It was signed 'Mother'.

'Breakthrough,' said Donoghue.

'Sir?'

Donoghue skimmed the letter across the desktop towards Montgomerie, who read it and nodded.

'Want me to get on it, sir?'

'Yes, if you would.' Donoghue lit his pipe. 'It's not a two-hander, go and see what you can dig up and then do the formal identification number. Never pleasant, but it has to be done.'

Montgomerie stood and left Donoghue's office, pulling the door gently shut behind him.

The money, Stephanie Craigellachie's night's earnings, a Cellophane packet which once contained smack, now empty. So had she run out, was she strung out and biting through the flesh of her fingers until her supplier showed? Donoghue handled the Cellophane packet with care; if they were in luck enough prints could be lifted to nail the pusher. Then there was the sour, ice-cold letter from 'Mother'.

Donoghue examined the wallet itself. It was old, of tooled leather, a man's wallet which opened like a book. He noticed the lining was torn. He pulled the lining away from the leather. There was a photograph inside, a colour print, showing a middle-aged man who looked to be about forty-five, he wore light trousers, black shirt, he seemed to have a gold medallion hanging around his neck. He had golden hair which he had combed over his scalp from left to right as if to cover a bald patch. He had his arm round a blonde-haired girl of perhaps thirty years. Maybe more. She was dressed cheaply. Too tight skirt for her years. Too tight and too short. The photograph was taken out of town, though clearly somewhere in the West of Scotland.

The couple were leaning against a black Mercedes. On the reverse a neat female hand had written 'Jimmy "the Rodent" and Toni, a week before she disappeared'. Also in the wallet, wedged in the corner, was a book of matches taken from a dive called Sylvester's.

'Breakthrough,' said Donoghue, 'breakthrough on all fronts.'

'Have you no got a copy of this?' asked the excited scratcher, holding up the photo. 'It's rare, so it is.'

'No,' said King.

'Sure?' He was a young man with black hair and keen eyes. 'It's rare, so it is.'

'Sure I'm sure.' King sat in the man's studio. Even to his untrained eyes it was noticeably more amateurish, more shoe-string and sealing-wax, than the first studio he had visited. Here there were cups full of dried ink, discarded gloves, a slight smell of sweat and all artificial light. 'I take it that you haven't seen this before?'

The man shook his head but continued to grin none the less. 'No,' he said eventually.

'So you didn't do it?'

The scratcher shot a keen glance at King. 'Do you think

I'd forget a job like this, pal? "I belong to Dino." Lucky old Dino, eh?'

'But you'd do something like that if someone asked?'

'Oh sure, sure, I'd tattoo them anywhere, if they want it they get it, any design anywhere. If they come in steaming drunk and want a pink butterfly put on the middle of their forehead, then they get it. If they don't think it was such a good idea in the cold light of day, then that's their problem. See, me I'm in business, I give the customer what he wants. If I didn't do it someone else would. Can't pay the tallyman if you turn good business down, my man.'

'Been in this game long?'

'Six months. I'm doing OK. Used to drive a taxi for the man, before that I was a steel erector. I fancied going it alone so I bought this equipment second-hand and set myself up.'

'No training?'

'Practised on oranges for a week, then I opened for business.'

'Keeping it clean I hope,' said King. 'Could be the environmental health could shut you down if they don't like what they see.'

The man shrugged. 'I give the place a good wash down with disinfectant every once in a while.'

'Every once in a while,' King echoed. 'So tell me, if you didn't do this do you know anyone who might have done it?'

'Bit blurred, isn't it,' said the man, 'the letters I mean, not the photograph, as clear as daylight is the photograph, sure you couldn't run me off a copy?'

'No chance.' King's voice hardened. 'Don't waste any time by asking again.'

'I've given them tattoos in some places, Jim, but never there . . .'

'So who might have?'

'You could try Old Fat Charlie,' said the scratcher. 'He's

got a place in the next street, looks a bit like a scrappies yard, gate and a corrugated iron fence.'

'They get worse,' said King.

The man handed King the photograph with noticeable reluctance.

King walked round to Old Fat Charlie's place. The houses in Bridgeton were dry, courtesy of summertime; in the winter he knew that he could do this same walk and smell the damp coming from the houses. But now it was summer, windows were open, music blasted loudly, children screamed in play, the communal front gardens filled up with rubbish, discarded cans of super lager and empty Buckfast Abbey wine bottles, hypodermic syringes, paper caked in dried glue. King found Old Fat Charlie's place without difficulty. It was as the young scratcher described, a hut behind a corrugated iron fence on which was painted 'Old Fat Charlie. Tattoo Artist'. King tried the gate. It was locked.

'He's no in.'

King turned. The owner of the voice was a derelict who sat slumped against the street lamp, feet in the gutter between two parked cars.

'When will he be in?'

The derelict shrugged and spat. 'Maybe tomorrow. Business is slow so he went to Delayney's.'

King looked at the iron fence. He wasn't surprised business was slow. He thought of Delayney's. He didn't know to which particular Delayney's bar Old Fat Charlie had gone but each was identical and each geared to nothing but hard drinking for men. Delayney's ran a string of bars, all of the same name, selling only cheap wines and spirits and short measures of either. King knew that if Old Fat Charlie had gone to a Delayney's bar he would be slumped against the gantry or leaning against a pillar, a glass of wine in one hand and glass of whisky in the other, enjoying oblivion and probably about to slide heavily on to the floor.

It was, King thought, hardly worth his while looking for him.

'Got ten pence for a cup of tea, sojer?' groaned the derelict.

King handed the man a fifty-pence piece. He didn't normally give money to down-and-outs but this time he did. The man had after all been of assistance to the police.

The couple surprised Montgomerie. And he disliked them.

The house first. He didn't like the house. At least he did not like the way it had been decorated. From the outside there was nothing to distinguish it from any other suburban box in Bearsden where as Karen had just that morning said, 'even the muggers say "please".' The house was a bungalow with a dormer window built into the roof, a room in what had been the attic. The building was of white-painted pebbledash with a yellow door. The street number was forged in wrought iron and fastened to the front of the house, and underneath the number was the name of the house, 'Clovelly', which was similarly fashioned out of wrought iron. The garden in front of the house was neat. Too neat really, close-cropped lawn, flowerbeds of dainty flowers, pansies particularly, a gravel drive down which two sets of flagstones were laid leading up to the garage door, and which were obviously carefully swept. Montgomerie thought that a weed growing in the flowers, or a pebble on the flagstones, could have been a welcome sight. There were of course the garden gnomes, two of them, and a miniature castle for them to sit beside, snugly among the pansies.

Montgomerie walked up to the door and pressed the bell. It played 'Auld Lang Syne' and brought two Pekinese yapping at the letter-box.

The inside of the house exuded the same feeling of fastidious neatness and obsession with trivia. The furniture was modern, light, not at all comfortable, and seemed to be somewhat scaled down in size. The pink carpet was wall to wall and deep pile. The television was allowed to protrude into the room. Mass-produced prints hung on the wall and the household possessed one that never failed to irritate Montgomerie: it showed the face of an angelic-looking child, round-eyed and with a tear running down his cheek. The room seemed to be dominated by items of idle amusement: a fish tank with fish and a sign in the gravel which said 'no fishing', a little menagerie of glass animals parading along the mantelpiece or grouped round the electric logs, a chrome-plated silver thing which seemed to Montgomerie to serve no purpose other than to spin slowly, silently, mesmerically. A cuckoo clock hung on the wall. There was of course no music playing, the house was as dry as death, and no sound from the outside. The double glazing saw to that.

The occupants next. The home owner and his wife. They were dressed neatly, he in a light-coloured shirt, a satin jacket, light trousers and cream and brown shoes. His thick leather belt with a heavy buckle seemed oddly out of place with the rest of his dress. He had a thin face, a good head of black hair, neatly combed. His lady wore a matching blue blouse and skirt, blue stockings and blue court shoes. Montgomerie asked if they were about to go out and apologized if his visit caused any inconvenience. No, they said, they were not going out, they were just sitting in this afternoon.

They were dressed to perfection, in a house kept to perfection and which was surrounded by a garden kept to perfection. They were not expecting him. They always lived like this . . . they always lived like this. Montgomerie became afraid of even clearing his throat.

He asked if he might sit down and after adjusting to the cramped and delicate feeling of the settee he inquired if they knew of one Stephanie Craigellachie.

'Our foster daughter,' said Mr Keys. He had a 'thin' voice. Menacing.

'Our only one,' echoed Mrs Keys. She had a whiny voice.

Thin and menacing and whiny. Montgomerie felt himself beginning to crawl up the wall. He regretted that he might have some bad news for them.

'How could she do this to us?' said Mr Keys when Montgomerie had explained the reason for his visit.

'After all we have done for her,' echoed Mrs Keys.

'She was always so selfish,' Mr Keys said.

'Very selfish,' said his wife.

Montgomerie thought she was in her mid-fifties, but could be hiding a lot of years under her make-up and hairdo. Her husband was clearly in his sixties but had a thin frame and carried the clothing of a thirty-year-old with only limited difficulty.

'She grew up here?' prompted Montgomerie when it became clear that the Keys were not only going to be unforthcoming with emotion and information, but were also quite happy, it seemed, to sit in silence staring at each other, basking in each other's attention, which was, presumed Montgomerie, how they spent their days, cop or no cop on the settee.

'Yes,' said Mr Keys.

'Yes,' said Mrs Keys.

Another silence. Montgomerie knew he was going to have to work hard.

'How long did she live with you?'

'We rescued her from an awful children's home which was full of rattling cutlery and yelling children when she was ten years old.' Mr Keys gazed at his wife.

'Ten years old,' said Mrs Keys.

Montgomerie suddenly realized that the Keys kept looking at each other even when speaking to him. He wondered with a sudden sense of fear and unease if it had been like this when Stephanie was growing up here? 'How was school today?' would ask Mrs Keys of her husband as Stephanie walked into the room.

'We brought her here.'

'Here,' echoed Mrs Keys.

'And we brought her up as it was our Christian duty to do so.'

'Our duty.'

You are not ringing true, thought Montgomerie. You are not ringing true at all.

Then there was a silence again. Just the rapid and faint ticking of the cuckoo clock provided any sound. The only movement in the room was the small silver thing which went round and round and round. The Keys sat in a virtually catatonic state, gazing across the room into each other's eyes. Thirty seconds passed.

'It will be necessary for one of you at least to attend the mortuary and identify the body,' said Montgomerie when it became clear the Keys were not interested enough to ask any questions, and to break the silence, and to take his mind off the mesmeric spinning toy.

'I will do that,' said Mr Keys.

'My husband will do that,' said Mrs Keys.

'She was stabbed,' said Montgomerie. 'Just to warn you that there will be a wound on the neck which could be visible. Usually they just expose the face and nothing else.'

'We wondered when you were going to tell us how she died,' said Mrs Keys.

'Well, now you know,' Montgomerie said testily. 'Do you know much about her lifestyle?'

'Little,' said Mr Keys.

Mrs Keys remained silent.

'Did you meet any of her friends? We are particularly keen to trace a man called "Dino" who could be a man or a woman, but we are inclined to think it's a male.'

'Why?' Mr Keys glanced momentarily at Montgomerie and then returned his gaze to his wife.

Montgomerie faltered, searching for an answer. He faltered because not only was the question unexpected given the impression Montgomerie was forming of the couple, but it was difficult to know how to describe the tattoo, especially its location on their foster-daughter's anatomy, and especially to the Keys who had up to that moment seemed so prim and twee. But he also faltered because the question had been thrown with a sharpness and a quality of accusation which had caught him off guard, and moreover when Keys looked at him Montgomerie looked into the man's eyes, and just for a second, a split second, he glimpsed the man's soul.

The man was evil.

'I'd rather not say,' said Montgomerie, beginning to feel a worm of doubt and fear growing in him, a fear of being in a potentially dangerous situation; this perfect Legoland house was in fact fraught with danger. Mr Keys was not to be underestimated, the very core of his personality was demonic. Montgomerie looked at Keys who was once again sitting still looking adoringly at his wife, all in blue. Montgomerie wondered whether or not he had seen the look in the man's eyes. He decided that he had.

Keys grunted an acceptance of Montgomerie's explanation.

'So,' said Montgomerie, 'did Stephanie mention a Dino to you at all?'

'Not at all,' said Keys.

'Never,' said his wife.

'Do you know where she lived?'

'Yes,' said Keys. 'We have her address.'

'In Kelvinbridge,' said Mrs Keys.

'Did you visit?'

'No.'

'No.'

'If you had, I think you would have found it a little different from your home here,' said Montgomerie.

No response. The Keys evidently expected an explanation would be forthcoming and seemed prepared to wait for it. They were, as they had said, sitting in for the afternoon and in no hurry. The cuckoo clock ticked and the chrome thing went round and round and the fish tank bubbled.

'She didn't have a great deal of money,' said Montgomerie.

'She told us that she was unemployed,' Keys said in what was to be the only unsolicited statement he made.

'She was in a sense.' Montgomerie grasped the opportunity for a rapport. 'In that she was not employed as such. She was drawing benefit as an unemployed person but she was bringing in much more money than I do each week.' Mrs Keys looked up, caught her breath and proved that she was capable of independent thought.

'Oh, sir, you're not suggesting she was a criminal, or worse . . . not one of those girls who stand in Blythswood Street.'

'The second, I'm afraid,' said Montgomerie.

Mrs Keys pulled out a small handkerchief with flowers embroidered on the corner and rushed out of the room fighting back tears.

'You've upset my wife,' said Keys coldly, flatly, unemotionally, but not moving an inch, not even taking his eyes from the chair his wife had been occupying, content it seemed to wait for her eventual return.

CHAPTER 5

Wednesday, 16.00–19.30 hours

Sussock left his flat and walked down to Byres Road. He bought something sticky and unsubstantial from a fast food joint and then he walked back and washed the grease from his hands. He fixed himself a coffee and drove to the other side of the water, to Rutherglen. He didn't relish the prospect of the visit he was to make. He told himself that he ought to be used to it by now, he'd had occasion to call back once a week or ten days since he had walked out, months ago, right in the middle of the Glasgow Knife Murders case as he recalled, when snow lay deep and cruel in the very dead of winter. At the age of fifty-five years he walked out of his marriage, at an age when couples should be enjoying each other's company with their life's work and child-rearing behind them. But not him, he'd walked and he still felt the wonderful sense of pressure being suddenly lifted from his shoulders. His leaving had been sudden, spontaneous, impetuous, and he had to call back frequently to the bungalow he had shared with the lady who was his wife in name only. All too frequently for comfort.

In Rutherglen he drew up in front of a modest bungalow, left his car, walked up the drive and hammered on the door of the building. He was in no mood for diplomacy. The house was in silence but he knew the routine. He knew it line well. He could picture them, upon his knock throwing a glance at each other and possibly sniggering. Perhaps they even saw him coming up the drive and Sammy would say, 'Quick, Mummy, it's him. Let's hide and pretend we're not at home.' They might even have crawled quickly underneath the dining-room table together.

So he hammered on the door again. This time he succeeded in raising a howl from the interior. Then he heard footsteps inside the house and approaching the front door. The key turned in the lock and then his son's mincy voice called out, 'Who is it?'

'You know fine well who it is,' snarled Sussock. 'Just open the door.'

The door opened but only after a needling pause. Samuel stood there, tall, thin, two rings in his left ear and his jersey, even in summer he wore a jersey, was tucked into the waist of his baggy trousers. 'Hello, Daddy,' he said. Sussock started up the steps and pushed passed him. Samuel cowered needlessly.

'Is it him?' a piercing female voice wailed from the sitting-room.

'Yes, Mummy,' Samuel replied as he ran behind Sussock with hurried little footsteps.

The woman flew out of the room. She was small and pinched-faced. She glared at Sussock as they confronted each other in the hallway. 'What are you doing here? You! You were never interested in me or Sammy, was he, Sammy, never at home, out catching robbers all the time and drinking with his mates . . . and . . . and . . .'

But Sussock just turned and went to a small room where all his possessions had been dumped. He raked through the collection of cardboard boxes and collected items of summer clothing which he stuffed into a plastic bag. Samuel stood in the doorway with one hand on his hip. 'Why don't you take it all, Daddy, or is your flat not big enough? I've a boyfriend who's looking for a room, and Mummy likes him too.'

'Not be long now,' said Sussock icily.

'Not be long before what, Daddy?'

'Not be long before it's all finalized. Not be long before the divorce is through, then I can instruct my solicitor to raise an action for division and sale. Sell the house, pay off the balance of the mortgage and split the proceeds with that thing in there. Then you'll be on your own and I mean your own.'

'Oh, Daddy,' Samuel smiled. 'You're so handsome when you're angry.'

Sussock left the house in a cold fury. He drove thankfully to Langside, calming with each turn of the wheels. The tension he had built up inside him prior to the encounter with his wife and son was now leaving him in waves. In Langside he pulled up outside a close and climbed the stair. Three up he came to a door, on the right, with 'Willems' inscribed in gold on a fancy tartan nameplate, just above the letter-box. He rang the doorbell.

She opened it. Her hair was let down, long and golden, to her shoulders. She wore a rugby shirt of green and yellow in horizontal stripes, figure-hugging stonewashed denims, and trainers. She smiled and said, 'Hi. Hi, old Sussock,' and hooked her finger under the knot of his tie and pulled him gently into her flat. 'I expected you this morning. You're late.'

He kissed her. 'Just felt too tired when I got in,' he said. 'I flaked out. Couldn't phone.'

She rotated him and hipped the door shut. 'Thought that was what had happened. You're forgiven, old Sussock.'

Later as he lay alone in her bed he looked around the room. Elka Willems's flat was tastefully decorated, he had always thought so. It was painted in pastel shades, books on shelves, a Van Gogh print on the wall. Her flat was a 'room and kitchen', just one room and a kitchen, an ideal-sized flat for one person living alone, but it had originally been intended as a family home and Sussock had in fact grown up in such a flat in the old Gorbals, the 'old town', as one of seven children, sharing the one bed with their parents, spilling on to the floor as they grew older, nits in their hair, shorn and daubed by the medical officer, lice in their clothing, parents passing coal gas through milk as a cheap and effective intoxicant, or drinking the lethal 'red biddie', the screams in the night and in the morning the pool of dried congealed blood on the common stair. Sussock was well aware that some people, many people in fact, had fond memories of the old Gorbals but he was not one of them, not being at all sorry to see them come down. In their place the city had erected three huge high-rise tower blocks and if duty ever took him there he'd often take time out, answering a tug, to walk over the old ground. The street pattern of the old Gorbals largely remained, as do some of the old bars on Pollokshaws Road, but apart from the tower blocks the site was now a waste ground with the new Sheriff

Court, 'the busiest in Europe', to the north, the railway viaduct to the south, main drags to east and west. On a winter's day it was a desolate and bleak square mile.

That was the Gorbals. This was Langside, summertime, warm, well ordered, clean vacuumed, wood polished, with Mozart playing on the hi-fi.

She came into the room. He loved to see her naked, so perfectly formed, everything in proportion.

'Two coffees,' she said with a tone of disapproval in her voice.

'Well, it'll be wine after this run at night shifts.'

She bent down and placed his mug on the bedside cabinet. As she turned away he gave her bottom a playful slap. She yelped 'Ouch!' and smiled and carried her coffee across the floor and stood in front of the tall windows, looking out on to the street below. Net curtains hid her from view but allowed her to gaze out at Langside.

Sussock leaned up in the bed sipping his coffee. He looked at her. He couldn't take his eyes off her and her form was such that she kept the eye moving. He thought her perfect, from the front, from the side and as in this case from behind. And still just twenty-seven years old.

Then he lay back and looked at the ceiling which he had repainted for her at the very beginning of the summer. He thought of the women in his life, the shrew in Rutherglen, the Nordic goddess in Langside who was young enough to be his daughter and who hadn't come quietly, officer. The absurd black and white of it.

Montgomerie drove Leopold Keys to the GRI. He escorted him to the mortuary, walking in the bowels of the huge hospital, thick industrial lino, pipes running along the roof of the corridor, doors set back, some with radio-activity warning signs on them.

He opened the door to the mortuary and entered the ante-room. The attendant stood as they entered.

Montgomerie showed his identification. He said, 'Stephanie Craigellachie, please.'

The attendant nodded and showed them into the mortuary itself. He walked to a drawer, one of a bank of metal drawers set in the wall, and pulled it outwards. He parted the cloth which covered the face of the deceased, believed to be Stephanie Craigellachie.

'That is my foster daughter,' said Leopold Keys, with not the slightest trace of emotion that Montgomerie could detect.

Returning in the car, Montgomerie asked what sort of girl she had been.

'A difficult, wayward child.' Leopold Keys stared straight ahead as Montgomerie drove up Maryhill Road towards Bearsden. 'But we gave her a good home and did our duty as we saw fit.'

As we saw fit. Alarm bells began to ring in the distant recesses of Montgomerie's mind.

'When did she leave your home?'

'At sixteen,' said the impeccably dressed Leopold Keys.

'So early?'

'Well, she was never really happy in Bearsden. She came from Possilpark, if you see what I mean.'

'I don't,' said Montgomerie, grasping the opportunity to provoke some spontaneity in Keys.

'Well, there is a social gap,' said Leopold Keys. 'Stephanie never seemed to adjust to our ways. She was found by the police in a house in Possilpark when she was seven. Her parents had just left her there, turned the key and walked away. Never seen again. She was in the house for two days, no food, just tap water. Three years in a children's home toughened her up, she was swearing like a trooper when she came to us. We managed to knock off a few rough edges . . .'

Knock off a few rough edges. Again the warning bells sounded distantly.

'It was an uphill struggle. She was a street-smart, tough

little kid when we got her, no table manners, never cleaned her shoes unless she was really made to. She wore Mrs Keys into the ground.'

'You don't have children of your own?'

'No. We can't.'

'I'm sorry.'

'It's one of those things we have had to learn to live with. Stephanie was a challenge, more of a challenge than we bargained for. If we had been able to have her when she was younger it would have been easier, but by the time we got her she was set in her ways. A very obstinate girl.'

'What do you do?' asked Montgomerie.

'What do you mean?'

'What's your occupation?'

'Is that any of your business?'

'Yes,' said Montgomerie, 'it is.'

Leopold Keys paused. 'I have private means.'

'Meaning?'

'I made a killing on the stock exchange. Quite some years ago now. I have not needed to work for several years and I won't ever need to.'

In the Keys' household, in a pine-clad kitchen with rows of dainty cups hanging on the wall and decorated with oddments bought from souvenir shops, Leopold Keys said to his wife, 'It was her, Olive.'

And Olive Keys said, 'How could she do this? Doesn't she realize it reflects on us? She is so mean, so selfish, so inconsiderate.'

'We did what we could for her, Olive.' Leopold Keys spoke in a deadpan voice. 'Nobody can say we didn't.'

'You said earlier,' said Montgomerie, 'you said that she was a difficult child. What did you mean exactly?'

'Why do you ask?' Again the flat deadpan voice of Leopold Keys.

'It may be of relevance,' Montgomerie persisted.

'Well, she was untidy, dirty and slovenly,' Mrs Keys

hissed with indignation. 'She wouldn't clean her shoes.'

'Or brush her teeth.'

'We had to make her do those little things.'

'If she was going to be a lady.'

'It was an uphill struggle. No support, just a modest fostering allowance and left to get on with it.'

'She left when she was sixteen, I understand?' asked Montgomerie.

'Yes.'

'Yes.'

'Did she return, ever?'

'Not for any length of time,' said Mr Keys.

'A few days at the most,' said Mrs Keys.

'To pick things up.'

'Or drop things off.'

'Can I see her room?'

'If you must.'

'If you like.'

Leopold Keys took Montgomerie towards the rear of the bungalow. Mrs Keys followed. They walked on carpet of deep pile and they passed the main bedroom of the house. Montgomerie glanced inside, a modern pine four-poster bed, trimmed with lace, a blue carpet, modern furniture, a pine chest at the foot of the bed, and along one wall a row of female boots, all highly polished, Montgomerie guessed there were about twenty pairs.

Stephanie Craigellachie's room was at the rear of the house. It was a small room, the smallest in the house, thought Montgomerie. The floor was covered with thin linoleum, cracked and torn in places, the small bed was of inexpensive plywood, shoddily painted. One of the walls was covered in loud garish wallpaper, two were painted white, the wall against which the bed stood was bare plaster on which numerous games of noughts and crosses had been played and it seemed to Montgomerie to have been played with a lonely pencil. Most of the games were on that part of the wall closest to the pillow. A crate which once held oranges stood on the floor, inside which were some old books about horses and school holidays. A wardrobe without a door stood in the corner of the room. Poor, low quality clothing hung in the wardrobe.

'We haven't touched her room,' said Olive Keys. 'In case she should have wished to return.'

'Our door was never closed to her,' said Leopold Keys.

'She doesn't look too happy,' said the man in the flower-patterned shirt.

'She's not anything.' Donoghue recovered the photograph. 'She's dead.'

'Well, in that case I dare say she wouldn't be happy,' the man beamed. 'What was her name again?'

'Stephanie Craigellachie. You sure you haven't seen her?'

'Positive, Jim.'

'We found these among her possessions.' Donoghue tossed the book of matches on to the highly polished bar top between a beer cloth and an ashtray. Soft lights played on the spirit rack, soft music played in the background.

'They're ours right enough,' said the man turning the book of matches over and over in his hand. 'New, too.'

'Oh.'

'Aye, we changed the design. We've only been using this design for two weeks. The old design had "Sylvester's" printed in simple bold letters, the new design as you see here is like someone's handwriting. Also it's silver on black. The old design was white on black. So, if she was in here she must have been in the last fourteen days. We give them out free to anybody who buys cigarettes.'

'I see.'

'Nice-looking girl. I think I'd have remembered her if she had come in when I was serving. Work in the Square, did she, aye?'

'Just off.'

'Insurance executive? Bank clerk?'

Donoghue shook his head. 'The street,' he said. 'She worked the street.'

The man dropped the book of matches as if they were contaminated. 'Then she definitely wouldn't come in here. Definitely not. Was she the girl who was murdered the other night? I read it in the papers?'

'Last night, yes.' Donoghue looked at the man. The man's eyes had gone cold. He was not unlike most publicans of Donoghue's acquaintance, affable, superficially friendly, but liable to turn aggressive very rapidly. Donoghue enjoyed a good pub or a bar, but publicans were his least favourite group of people; constantly defending their territory.

'Take a hard line, do you?'

'Have to, Inspector,' said the man, mellowing, thawing again after the sudden flash of anger. 'They come in here, the expensive ones, one even has a full-length mink . . .'

'I think I met her,' said Donoghue. 'I thought she was in her mid-twenties, turned out she was nineteen.'

'They age,' said the barman, 'that's what gives them away. They have a worn or a used look. Most come from the schemes or from outlying towns, and even if they have a mink coat or other classy clothing they don't know how to carry it. They stick out like . . .'

'Vice girls in a smooth bar,' suggested Donoghue.

'Exactly.' The publican shot himself a tonic from the gun. 'Drink, sir?'

'Thanks,' said Donoghue. 'I'd like a tonic as well, from the bottle if you don't mind. Ice and lemon.'

'Just what you need on a day like this.' The barman fixed the drink. 'Good health,' he said, placing the drink on a new coaster. Donoghue thought he said 'good, elf'. 'No, I don't want this place to become a pick-up parlour.'

Donoghue glanced round him. It was the first time he had been in Sylvester's, a basement cocktail bar in Blythswood

Square, all velvet and chrome and soft music. The drinks were fifty per cent above normal city prices but the publican knew that mostly everyone who ate and drank at Sylvester's was on an expense account, so what the hell? The bar was used by businessmen from the Square, it did most of its trade at lunch-time, and according to the plaque outside, shut down at 9.30 each weekday night and shut completely from 9.30 Friday until 11.00 a.m. Monday. Civilized hours for any publican, early nights and every weekend off. Not bad. Donoghue took out the photograph which had been found in Stephanie Craigellachie's wallet. 'Seen this guy, or the girl?'

The barman leaned forward and tapped the photograph, 'Aye,' he said slowly, thoughtfully. 'Aye, now when did I see them?'

'In here? Together?'

'Aye,' he said. 'And not so long ago either. A week. Maybe two weeks. They had a meal. She on the game as well, this lassie?'

'We don't know.'

'I remember them well, see her she was so thin, built like a racing snake, but she was no anorexic, threw down her food like there was no tomorrow, a real wee snapper she was. Reminded me of my bears.'

'Your bears?'

'My weans, my children. My wife's blonde, see, so at home it's Goldilocks and the three bears. I love my bears, so I do, but see, trying to teach them table manners, it's unreal, so it is. Anyway she reminded me of them the way she shovelled her food in and tossed her knife and fork on the plate when she'd finished instead of placing them centrally. She was dressed well, brown outfit, went with her hair.'

'What was he like?'

'Small too. See this photograph, even though there's a motor to give some scale they somehow look bigger than they were in reality. He was a totty wee man but he swaggered when he walked.'

'Hard man?'

'Reckon he might have fancied himself as one. He was only about five feet six inches, maybe less if he had large heels. I know that men tend to be small in the West of Scotland, but even allowing for that he was on the small side all right. He was no businessman, black shirt with a gold medallion round his neck. Good head of hair for a man of his age. I'd put him at fifty.'

'Fifty?'

'Easy fifty. He dressed younger but he'll not see forty-five again. I don't think he'll see fifty again. There were lines round his mouth and eyes and he'd got chunks out of his cheeks, healed over as dead white skin, and he had a long scar on his forearm, all as though he'd fallen into a tube of razor blades. But he obviously didn't take the second prize all the time if only because he was still alive. He seemed to be a guy who had carved himself a slice of life the hard way.'

'I'm surprised that you served him.' Donoghue turned and glanced at a group of grey-suited executives leaving the premises, laughing together at a shared joke. 'I mean this man and the girl.'

'They were in and served before I'd properly clocked them. I didn't like them but they paid good money, didn't cause bother and went away happy. People like that pay my mortgage whether I like them or not and once in a while they do no harm, but too many of them and the place gets seedy and the downward spiral starts. I'd start to lose customers like the gentlemen who went up the stairs just now. Maybe I could turn over more money if I let the place get seedy in a flash sort of way, but I'm a family man and I have my bears to think about. One day they'll get to know what sort of gaff their dad runs and I'll have to look them in the eye. I've got to mind that day.'

'Very wise.'

'You a family man, sir?'

'Two,' said Donoghue, 'one of each, not started secondary school yet. At a nice age, old enough to talk to, young enough to need you.'

'Nice. Mine are all boys.'

'So this guy and female, you just saw them the once?'

'Aye.'

'About fourteen days ago?'

'Aye. That's the difficult part right enough, the days just fly in, merging with one another. Sometimes I forget what I did yesterday and other times I can remember events of months or years ago as clear as daylight.'

'It just means you've got a busy life.'

'I think it means that I'm suffering pre-senile dementia.'

'You never saw them separately?'

'No. The only reason why I clicked when I saw the photo is that I remember them like that, as a couple. Him swaggering about fighting the years and life, it seemed, and her younger and thinner and hungry. They stuck in my mind. He bought a cigar.'

'A cigar?'

'Yes. I remember. I get cynical at times, you know, I mind looking at him and wondering which hole in his face he was going to stick the cigar. He had a choice between his mouth and two or three others where a blade had torn chunks away. It doesn't show in the photograph but his face is like the surface of the moon. I gave him a book of matches.'

Donoghue asked, 'New or old?'

'New. I remember clearly. That pins it down to within the last fourteen days that they were here, very close to the beginning of the time that we started issuing the new style matches.'

Donoghue drained his glass and stepped nimbly off the

stool. 'Perhaps you'll let us know if they come in again, either as a pair or singly?'

'Anything to be public-spirited. Mind how you go.'

'You want me to wait outside?' asked Montgomerie. Collette smiled as she raised two pint tumblers on the rack underneath the gantry. 'If you don't mind, Malcolm. We're not allowed to entertain friends on the premises.'

'Am I only a friend?' He glanced at his reflection in the mirror behind the spirit rack. OK, so fate had been good to him, black hair, chiselled features, downturned moustache, he had enjoyed the longing looks of women of all ages since he was seventeen. He looked at Collette, a slim, trim, dark-haired child who wore the pink dress that was the uniform of the female staff of the Long Bar on Great Western Road. 'I thought I was more than that?'

'You know what I mean.' She glanced round and saw the tall, elegant manageress was still engrossed in an argument with a drunken customer about the bar prices. 'So where are you taking me tonight?'

Montgomerie shrugged. 'Where do you fancy?'

'I'm in your hands.' Then she went to serve a customer.

'Well, a drink,' he said when she returned, 'a meal and back to my place for a game of Scrabble.'

'Oh, that sounds like fun.'

'I'll be waiting for you across the road.' He pointed to another chrome and music and lights West End of Glasgow bar.

'Look forward to it. It'll be my last night out for four nights. Tomorrow, Thursday, I work a split and then I've got three night shifts.'

'Split?'

'Eleven till two, seven till eleven. It's murder.'

Later, over a meal in the Indian restaurant close to Montgomerie's flat just off Highburgh Road, he said, 'Cloying.'

'Cloying?' Collette looked up at him.

'Cloying.' He tore a piece of chapatti and scraped the last of the sauce from his plate. 'I had occasion to visit a house today, up in Bearsden, this couple lived there, late middle-aged, over-dressed, as though they were about to go out but they were just sitting in, there was a word I knew existed to describe their relationship but I couldn't think of it.'

'But it's "cloying"?'

Montgomerie nodded and tore off another piece of chapatti.

King sat in front of Donoghue's desk. He glanced out of the window at the evening settling like a comfort blanket over the rooftops of Glasgow town. It was still warm enough at this time of the night not to need a jacket out of doors, and warm enough indoors for Donoghue to have opened the windows of his office. Donoghue sat in his waistcoat and pulled on his pipe and considered. King returned his attention to the Inspector.

'I think I'd still like to find out who Dino is,' said Donoghue, 'but I can't help thinking that we are leading ourselves up a blind alley. Especially in the light of this information.' He tapped the file on the desk.

'I've located another so-called scratcher, sir. He was out bevvying when I called at his place of work. I think I'd like to call back tomorrow just for the sake of completion. After that, well . . .'

'Very good.' Donoghue liked King. He found the young detective-constable to have a strong sense of professionalism, of thoroughness, he always seemed willing to go the extra mile. He was a detective-sergeant in a detective-constable's clothing, comfortably in the frame for early promotion.

'When did we receive this new information, sir?'

'It was in my pigeonhole when I came back from Sylvester's just before you returned. As I said, Elliot

Bothwell has lifted prints from the Cellophane packet which had contained heroin, quite a massive amount if the packet was full of the stuff. The prints in question belong to a known felon, none other than one Jimmy "the Rodent" Purdue. Here's his file and a right evil ned he is too by the sound of it. Convictions for violent crime, done time in Peterhead and Shotts.' Donoghue handed the file to King. 'You'll see he's a knife man, going by his form, carves people for a living and finally murdered a girl.'

'So now he's peddling dope?'

'Either that or he's delivering it. A courier is the word they use, so I believe. Either way he's left enough dabs on what was once a large consignment of smack for us to be interested in him for reasons over and above any connection with the death of Stephanie Craigellachie. It was uncut heroin, pure as the driven snow.'

'So how did a girl like Stephanie Craigellachie get hold of that amount of heroin?'

'Well, that is what we have to find out, so this is where we earn our crust,' said Donoghue, beginning to see a slight fissure opening in the case, enough to get a purchase on and to lever it wider. 'Time to shovel work.'

'So we assume Dino and the Black Team are side issues,' said King, closing the file on Jimmy 'the Rodent' Purdue, 'just things that we turned up along the way.'

Donoghue pulled on his pipe. It had gone out. He lit it with his lighter before replying. It was the privilege of rank and one which King found intensely annoying. 'I don't think we assume anything, Richard. The Black Team may be nothing more than a group of female muggers and we'd be interested in them in their own right, those girls who work the street are vulnerable enough as it is without being rolled by their own alumni. On the other hand the Black Team might be up to their collective oxters in the death of Stephanie Craigellachie. The other issue which I haven't told you about is that the collator has come up with another gem or another spanner in the works, depending upon how you look at it, in the form of a file on Toni Durham.'

'Who?'

'The girl in the photograph found in Stephanie Craigel-lachie's wallet.'

'Oh yes.' King nodded. 'Jimmy the Rodent with Toni Durham some time, a week I think, before she disappeared.'

'That's it. Helps us pin down the date of the photograph. Toni Durham was reported missing seven days ago. Now if Stephanie Craigellachie took the photograph, then she must have known Toni Durham and Jimmy the Rodent socially . . .'

'Or professionally,' said King. 'If their profession is vice and drugs.'

'Or professionally.' Donoghue allowed himself to be corrected.

'Jimmy the Rodent runs a black Mercedes, it's here in the photograph, she was seen to show fear of a man in a black car. So the man who took her off the street and returned her with a black eye was Jimmy the Rodent, pictured here with Toni Durham.'

'So it appears,' said Donoghue, 'Jimmy the Rodent and Toni Durham were friendly enough to go for a drink and a meal together at Sylvester's about fourteen days ago, shortly before she disappeared. Toni Durham has convictions for opportuning and theft. I think the case is beginning to shape up. Jimmy the Rodent is a known felon, with convictions for murder and violence, especially for knife attacks, he's a known associate of a girl who has disappeared and was also known to a girl who was murdered, significantly by being stabbed. The girl who was murdered was a smack head and seemed to have the remains of a large amount of heroin on her person which had Jimmy the Rodent's dabs on. Smells, doesn't it?'

'Like a pile of rotting leaves,' said King.

'So we need to locate Jimmy the Rodent, have a chat with

him. Let's talk to the girls on the street. I'd like to know more about the Black Team, see if any of the girls might know where Toni could be, see if any of them knew Stephanie Craigellachie. I'll put Abernethy on it, he's on the back shift.'

'Toni,' said King, rising from his seat, 'will be in a shallow grave somewhere.'

'I think she will too,' said Donoghue. 'So it's a double murder.'

They lay side by side in Montgomerie's bed. They hadn't closed the curtains, three up and facing a swing park you don't need to, and they watched the sun slowly sink over the city. Montgomerie lay on his front, exhausted, Collette again having been 'exciting', like he thought, a fish out of water, with screams. She now sat propped up against the headboard smoking a cigarette.

'You always been a cop?' she asked.

'More or less,' he said sleepily.

'Meaning what?'

'Meaning I read law at Edinburgh. Was going to practise.'

'What, until you got it right?'

'That joke is so old that it's pushing up daisies.' Frankly he'd never thought it that funny in the first place.

'So why didn't you . . . er . . . practise?'

'Didn't like lawyers.' He closed his eyes. Sleep wasn't too far away. 'Smug, self-satisfied bunch of people. I met people who were quite open about the fact that they were studying law for the sole reason that nobody ever meets a poor solicitor. People like that far outnumbered those who had a committed interest in the law and wanted to study and apply it.'

'I suppose,' she said. 'But is that so different from me saying that I'm studying History because I want to take the sugar boat?'

'I don't understand.'

'It's a Greenock expression,' she said, 'comes from the days when sailing ships used to bring sugar cane from the West Indies to the refinery at Greenock and then go away again for another load. If somebody leaves town we still say that they've taken the sugar boat. I wanted to take the sugar boat, so I studied History. The subject doesn't matter so long as I got a ticket on the boat. I mean, the only thing to do in Greenock is to get drunk and make babies. There's no work.'

'That's different,' he said. 'That's surviving. The guys that forced me out of Edinburgh were into nest-feathering. I came back to Glasgow because I love the city and became a cop because I care about people.'

He felt her run the tips of her fingers down his spine, but all he could think of was a small room with a broken bed, a box full of books, and games of noughts and crosses pencilled on the wall.

CHAPTER 6

Wednesday, 20.00–23.00 hours

'I'm a woman,' said the cigarette-smoker, standing on the corner, shoulder-bag, long hair. 'We run against time. Time presses heavily on us.'

'We just don't seem to have so many years to play around with as men have,' said the second. Abernethy thought she had a hard face.

'I think I knew Stephanie,' said the first, the cigarette-smoker. She dragged hard on the nail and blew the smoke out in a plume.

'We think she used to stand in the alley, just over there,' said Abernethy, feeling the women advancing on him.

'Aye, that's her,' said the first. 'She was—what? Early twenties? Time was running out for her. If she didn't break out soon she never would. She was heading for the bus station.'

'Or the Green,' said the second.

'Ugh!' The first shuddered.

'What do you know about her?' Abernethy looked southwards, down the length of Blythswood Street, concrete and glass, older buildings south of the water, hills beyond. His sports jacket was tugged by a warm breeze.

'She was filled in yesterday,' said the first, 'found in an alley with her throat slit from ear to ear. It's the talk of the street.'

'What do you know about her when she was alive?'

'She was OK,' said the second. 'She'd come down and talk at the end of the night.'

'Down where?'

'The corner down there. About one in the morning, we meet up, smoke a few cigarettes, after it gets quiet. We talk about what sort of night we've had, maybe spread the money about.'

'Spread it about?'

'Aye. I mean if one girl's been rolled by a punter, had her money nicked, we'd chip in a tenner each, especially if she was earning so she'd pay it back easily enough. It's a dangerous job, this, nearly as dangerous as being a cop. See, there's nowhere for us to stash our takings, so at the end of the night we'd be getting into cars with strange men with a good few hundred quid in our handbags. At that time of night there's a fair chance the punter is after your money and not your body. That's the first time I ever got talking to Stephanie. Everything had gone wrong for me that night and I mean everything, first a condom burst on me, then there was the guy who wanted me to act like a ten-year-old girl; I wouldn't, so he bounced my face off the dashboard of his car a couple of times. Then at the end of a long night I was driven on to a piece of waste ground south of the river, rolled and had my money stolen.'

'Well, they say things happen in threes,' said the second.

'You're really helpful at times,' said the first. Then she addressed Abernethy. 'So I went back to the street, found the girls in a group, told them what had happened and saw Stephanie. I'd never met her before, but she was the first to dip into her bag. Nice girl she was.'

'So she usually stopped about one in the morning.'

'Yes.'

'Some girls drag it out till five in the morning but they tend to start later. Stephanie started at about six in the evening and finished at one in the morning. She'd swap notes and listen. In fact she was the one who told me about the violent guy in a fancy car.'

'Aye, I was there,' said the second. 'She said just watch for him and don't get in his car.'

'What sort of car?'

'American. A big cream-coloured American car. Couldn't mistake it. See, Stephanie had got in and this guy had given her a good doing. He didn't take her money, he just slapped her around a good bit because he didn't like working girls. Stephanie warned us about him. See, some girls are dead spiteful, some girls would take a doing like that and say nothing, just stand there watching other girls getting into the same car and knowing exactly what's going to happen to them, thinking: If I had to take it, she can too. But not Stephanie, she wouldn't be like that.'

'So what happens after you've been attacked? Do you report it to us?' Both girls shook their heads. 'No point. Your word against his, no witnesses, you don't know his identification anyway. If you've got away with your life then pick yourself up, have a good drink, put it down to experience and start work again.'

'I see. Stephanie, she never talked about a man called Dino? Possibly it's a woman but we think it's a man.'

'Dino?'

'Dino?'

'Not to me,' said the first.

'Me neither. She did talk about a man, though.'

'Oh?'

'Aye. Seemed to be her angel,' volunteered the second.

'Angel?'

'Some girls have got angels, you know men they're either good or bad, it's hoping that you meet a good one that keeps girls going. See, the street, it's amazing how it brings out the good and bad in men.'

'You mean the God Squad,' said the first. 'There's as many women in that as men.' She dragged hard on the nail.

'No, not them.'

'Who are they anyway?' asked Abernethy.

'Religious nuts who are locked down tight with Jesus, they come on to the street each Friday evening handing out religious tracts, wanting us to go to church on the Sunday. It's all very well but singing hymns never paid the rent.'

'Or your supplier,' said Abernethy and both girls fell silent. 'So tell me about the good guys.'

'Well, there's the guys that beat you up and steal your money, and there's the queer hawks that want you to play games and then there are the guys who want to protect you.'

'Pimps?'

'No, no,' said the first, who seemed to Abernethy to like to be doing all the talking. 'I don't mean that. See, I've got an angel, he's a businessman. He comes to Glasgow from England, two sometimes three times a month. The first time he came looking for a girl to take to dinner. Sometimes it pays to be well-dressed because there's a chance you'll get offered a meal. You get these guys, middle-aged, got a bit of money, all they want is female company. They'll pay you to let them take you for a meal. It tends to bring out the protectiveness in them, the father figure bit. My angel looks me up when he's in town and hands me a wedge of smackers and says, "Right, that's you off the street for the next two nights." He offered me a job in his company.'

'Why didn't you take it?'

The girl shrugged. 'I'd feel I was exploiting him; you know—exploiting his goodness.'

'You feel you're not good enough to deserve a break in life?' asked Abernethy.

The girl looked at him with widening eyes and he knew he'd touched a raw nerve.

'I've got an angel too,' said the second. 'He wants to marry me. I remind him of his late wife.'

'So you think Stephanie had an angel?'

'Yes. She talked about him, never mentioned his name, though.'

'I see.' Abernethy nodded. He had been surprised by the girls. He had not really known what to expect, he'd seen them on the occasions they were lifted and taken to the 'tank', held for a few hours and charged with opportuning, and because of that he had anticipated aggression and hostility. In the course of events he had to admit to himself that they were nice girls, they were, really nice. At least the ones he had talked to had been pleasant young women. He had been strolling up and down Blythswood Street for an hour and a half talking to the girls, some who had known Stephanie and some who hadn't. They had all proved pleasant girls but it became apparent to Abernethy that they all had one thing in common: not one had a good self-image. It didn't seem to be a self-image that was brought about by the way they had chosen to earn a living, it was much more deeply rooted, already well-established and entrenched. The girls had seemed to gravitate to the street and to being exploited, as if to reinforce an opinion that they were there to be used if not abused, like this girl who didn't think she deserved a break in life. None the less, they were pleasant, Abernethy had to admit that, they were courteous, even if their speech was hard they still possessed essential courtesy. If they didn't value themselves, they did value other people. What had seemed to him to be a daunting task as he approached the Square had in fact turned out to be a pleasant assignment.

He said, 'She knew a man with a black Mercedes?'

'Yes, she did,' said the first girl. 'And he was no angel, take it from me.'

'Gave her a doing over,' said the first.

'I saw it.'

'The assault?'

'No. I saw him draw the car to a stop, wait for her. Leave the car and pull her in when she came. I was a good distance away but other girls were nearer and saw it more clearly. She was on the street the next night wearing dark glasses and not being able to speak properly. He'd slapped her around a good bit.'

'What did he look like?'

'He was a cocky little hard man,' said the first, 'stocky but solid, good head of hair.'

'I saw him around,' said the second. 'He'd been scarred, like lumps had been torn from his face.'

'She never mentioned him.'

'Never.'

'Did she have a pimp?'

'No.' The first girl tossed away the dog-end and pulled another nail from the packet and lit it with a gas lighter. 'Some girls do, most don't. There's guys they come up the street, just been made redundant, offer to watch your back for ten per cent of your takings. You tell them to get on their bikes, I mean how can they watch your back when you're a mile away in somebody's car. Mind you, once they get their claws into you then you're hooked for good. Bit like the money-lenders, once you say "yes" you're finished.'

'But there was nobody watching Stephanie's back?'

The girls shook their heads.

'Was the Black Team into her?'

There was a silence.

'The Black Team is into everybody,' said the second, finally.

'They rolled you?'

'Yes. Once. I can recognize them now so I get off my mark.'

'You'll need to point them out to us,' said Abernethy.

The girls shook their heads. 'I don't want any more doings than necessary. They're real hard women. Besides, if you get rid of them there's others that will move into their place. Women like that grow like weeds on this hill.'

'That's no reason to let them carry on with impunity. It's robbery with violence. Do you know if Stephanie ever got rolled by the Black Team?'

'Probably,' said the first.

'She did,' said the second.

'She did?'

'Yes, a few weeks ago. I saw it. All over in a few seconds, she was on the ground, her wedge lifted and the Black Team on their way before she knew what was happening. They didn't have it in for her any more than anyone else, she was just in the wrong place at the wrong time. It happens.'

'It happens,' Abernethy echoed. He was a young cop, early twenties, still a trace of residual acne. 'It happens,' he said again. 'All right, I have another question.'

'Come on,' the first protested. 'You're costing us money.'

'I won't detain you long,' said Abernethy. 'Toni Durham. Does the name mean anything to you?'

'Yes,' both girls said at once.

Abernethy raised an eyebrow after the manner of DI Donoghue when waiting for an explanation or an answer, but he hadn't Donoghue's silent charisma and both girls smiled at the gesture. So Abernethy said, 'Tell me what you know.'

'Haven't seen her for some time.'

'Two weeks or so.'

'What else do you know about her?'

'Wouldn't like to say.'

'Well, we can talk here or we can talk in the detention room.'

'OK, but this didn't come from us. OK?'

'Agreed.'

'And we're not giving evidence against her.'

'But we'll point you in the right direction.'

'Agreed.'

'Toni Durham,' said the first girl, 'she's a Miss Fix-it.'

'She's behind everything the scene has to offer.'

'The scene?'

The girl tapped her foot on the flagstones. 'The scene,' she repeated, 'the hill, the streets, the massage parlours, films . . .'

'Films?'

'Films, a room, a few lights, a video camera, a system for duplicating films, a few extras like a bed, maybe a tawse, a whip made out of suede and people to act. Adults, children when you can get them.'

Abernethy stood in shocked silence.

'You didn't know it was going on?'

'Not personally,' Abernethy conceded. 'I imagine Vice knows what's going down.'

'Well, you get asked to work as extras,' said the first girl. 'They pay more if the action's for real, whether you're in for a sore arse or two men at once, anything. They have a studio in Scotstoun.'

'Scotstoun?'

'Aye. Big tenement. Don't ask me where exactly. I was taken there by car, told to keep my eyes down or I wouldn't be seeing anything at all. I really needed money at the time so I agreed to do real action and had to sleep on my front for the next few nights. Never again.'

'They do films for gays,' said the second. 'They use boys who are on the run from List "D" Schools, they keep them hidden from the law, feed them, give them smokes. The boys call it "flogging their doughnuts".'

Abernethy's mouth opened. He was still inexperienced enough to be surprised by human behaviour. 'So what part has Tony Durham in that?'

'She's a talent scout looking for likely actresses. Offers you maybe a good night's money for two hours' filming. You don't need an Equity card to get into her films.'

'She never acts herself. The big money is to be made behind the scenes.'

'Do you know where she stays?'

'No.'

'No,' said the second. 'We can't answer too many questions, she could fix us so we couldn't work.'

'She could fix us period.'

'So we haven't talked to you about Toni Durham, OK?'

'Understood,' said Abernethy, 'but thanks.'

Abernethy glanced down the street. At the corner of St Vincent Street he noticed a man, a middle-aged man, talking to a girl. The man then glanced up the street to where Abernethy stood and the two men caught each other's gaze for a second. Abernethy hoped he never ended up like the man, middle-aged, lonely, buying your women for an hour in the evening, standing there negotiating price on the hoof in the Blythswood Street meat market. The older man looking at Abernethy thought it sad, such a young man should be negotiating with two girls. He turned back to the girl and said, 'Well, if you should see her, just tell her Dino was asking after her.'

Richard King arrived home late. He let himself in through the rear doorway. He heard Ian crying upstairs. It was a difficult time for Rosemary. Not only was Ian teething, but he was suffering badly from colic. He walked into the kitchen past the wood he had bought from the timber merchant the previous November with every good intention of putting up the shelves Rosemary had once requested and which she never reminded him about. He sat in his armchair and picked up that day's copy of the *Independent*, scanned the headlines but was too tired to read. Rosemary came downstairs quietly, unhurriedly, gentle in her presence as befitted her Quakerism. She was a slim girl, wore her hair in a bun, favoured pastel shades for her clothing and wore only skirts or dresses, never jeans or slacks. She laid her hand on his and said, 'Hello, we are pleased you are home.' She went to the kitchen and returned moments later with a mug of tea which she pressed into his hand. He pulled her towards him and kissed her gently. She smiled, she said dinner would be ready soon, it was just a question of heating it up.

In Edinburgh, in a suburban development of new housing of small front and rear lawns, with Volvos and smaller 'second' cars in the driveways, a man drove down the street. He was well dressed and smoked a pipe as he steered his Rover slowly and steadily towards a four-bedroomed bungalow. Inside the house a woman was baking, her daughter stood beside her kneading dough. Her son played with his model train in the adjacent room. The man entered the bungalow, the woman threw a powdery arm round her husband's neck, the children grabbed a leg each.

Fabian Donoghue had returned home.

Sussock leafed through the file on Jimmy 'the Rodent' Purdue. The photograph first, a hard sullen look, full face, three-quarter turn, profile. The file gave his height as five feet four inches tall, build was described as 'stocky', name James Maxwell Purdue, also known as 'the Rodent'. The given date of birth put his age at present at fifty-three. The list of previous convictions stretched to three sheets. He did a pen portrait of the convictions, a simple technique for summing up a character, convictions for violence and theft from the age of fifteen to twenty-seven, fines and sentences

of up to four years until finally at the age of thirty-one
Purdue was nailed for murder and served ten years. He
came out of the slammer at the age of forty-one and was not
heard of again. Until now, until the death of Stephanie
Craigellachie and the disappearance of Toni Durham. In
the last twelve years James Purdue had either gone straight
or committed crime undetected. Sussock sipped his coffee.
The latter he thought was the more likely.

He stood and crossed the floor of his office and glanced
out of the window. It was 10.00 p.m., just after, the city was
slumbering in a deep twilight. The lights within his office
caused his reflection to appear on the windowpane. He
looked at himself. Tall, thin, greying, fifty-five years of age.
He felt himself to be slowing up, a rapid deceleration.
Sussock returned to his desk. There was no information in
the file less than twenty-plus years old, other than copies
of prison reports and a note advising of his release from
Peterhead. None the less the photograph in the file and the
photograph of the man leaning against the black Mercedes
were definitely photographs of the same man, younger and
resentful-looking in the police files, older and more smug-
looking in the other photograph, but the same man all
right.

Sussock pulled the reports from the file and read in detail
the crimes he had been convicted for, a carving of a face, a
'Glasgow Kiss' with a broken bottle, breaking into cars; it
was, though, tame stuff by comparison. He put the reports
back into the file, leaned back in his chair and clasped his
hands behind his head. He had one large advantage over
any other cop who might read the file because it did not
seem like yesterday when he, still a detective-constable, was
part of a team which followed a bear of a man with no brain
across the city for a period measured in months, following
the man's spoor which seemed to consist of human blood
and dismembered bodies and skulls shattered like eggshells.
And did they pin any of it on him? Did they ever. The name

of bear with no brain: Jimmy 'the Rodent' Purdue. The file on Sussock's desk was playschool compared to what was down to Purdue but which could not be proved.

A man carved in front of his wife and kids, every muscle slashed through never to heal again. Total cripple.

That was Purdue.

A man crucified on the floor of a derelict tenement which was then set on fire. Sussock had attended the scene in time to hear the last of the screams from within the flames.

Later he attended the Forensic Science Laboratory and was shown two six-inch nails blackened and twisted in the heat.

That was Purdue.

There was the young pregnant woman found naked in the snow, kicked to death.

That was Purdue.

There was the woman with ninety-seven stab wounds.

That was Purdue.

That was just the tip of the iceberg. There were lots of busted limbs, and heads, lots of scars, lots of splints, plaster casts, and plasma drips.

And it was all down to Purdue.

Then he was nailed.

Sussock recalled how it happened. Purdue had taken a girl for a drink in a bar in the south side, just off Pollokshaws Road: it was a real dive. Had been a nice bar in its day, solid walnut, rich panelling, frosted glass, then it got a lazy manager, went down the tubes and by the time Purdue took the girl there it was just no place to take a lady. If he'd taken her to another bar things might have worked out for her, but as it was he was a hard man with scars on his face which he wore like medals and there's only one sort of bar a guy like that drinks in, lady or no lady on his arm. She had just six hours to live from the moment they found floor space to stand.

There was a tap on Sussock's door. It was opened before he could say anything. Elka Willems stood in the doorway, smiling, a mug of steaming tea in her hand.

'You're rich,' he said leaning forward, resting his elbows on his desktop.

'How do you mean?' She advanced and placed the mug of tea on his desk.

'Well, you're always going on about the need for discretion and here you are bringing me a mug of tea in the middle of a shift in full view of everybody.'

'In full view of nobody, old Sussock. Things are quiet down there, there's nobody up here. Abernethy's still out, not finished his shift yet. The others are off duty. What are you reading?'

'It's the file on Jimmy "the Rodent" Purdue.' He closed the file and handed it to her. 'Turns out that he might be involved in the murder of Stephanie Craigellachie. You visited her flat yesterday.'

'Oh yes.' She opened the file. 'Any progress?'

'Nothing to speak of. We'd like to trace this guy.' He tapped the file. 'There is the possibility that another girl who has been reported missing is caught up in it, one Toni Durham. She's a known associate of both Stephanie Craigellachie and Jimmy Purdue.'

'Murdered or missing?'

'Who can tell,' said Sussock, picking up his tea. 'She may have upped and gone to live in London, she may have fallen into the Clyde.'

'Or she may have been murdered by Jimmy the Rodent and her body concealed.'

'That wouldn't surprise me in the slightest,' said Sussock. 'I knew this turkey years ago.'

'Oh?'

'He's a pure animal, a violent wee thug, a knife-man.'

'That's significant. Stephanie Craigellachie was knifed.'

'It's only superficially significant.' Sussock held the mug

of tea with both hands. 'Her injury had the feel of a lucky stab wound and the knife was left in the body.'

'You don't think that's the work of Purdue?'

Sussock shook his head. 'He's a professional. If that was his work, then he was disturbed.'

'So there's a witness to the murder in the town, somewhere?'

'If the murder was down to Jimmy the Rodent, then yes, and it would have to be someone he was afraid of. It's something that I'll have to float with Fabian in the morning.'

'What's this?' Elka Willems pulled a sheet of paper from the file.

'It's his submission to the Parole Board,' said Sussock.

Elka Willems looked at it. The front sheet was in longhand, written in heavy deliberate printing, very legible but semi-literate. Attached were a number of photocopies each of which had a typed version also attached for the convenience of the Parole Board members. She read it.

I took Mandy for a wee drink. I took her to a bar in the south side. I had a heavy with a whisky. I told him to stick a head on the heavy. I was drinking all night. She looked at other men. We had a wee fight in the pub. I chibbed her with a broken glass and cut her neck. It wasn't me that did it, it was the drink. I took her out. Some guys followed. I still had the broken glass, I said I'd chib them too if they didn't back off. I flagged a cab and put Mandy in. I got in and said Rutherglen. The cab drove off. Mandy was making sounds. The driver said Mandy was sick and stopped. We got out. I chucked him a quid and told him he'd seen nothing but he must have told the polis because the streets were soon crawling with them looking for us. I got Mandy to a hut where I thought we could stay. She was moaning but I had my hand over her cut and I was letting her lean on me. We got to the hut and the man said we had to go so I said I knew where there was another hut where we could stay. She kept saying she was cold. I told her to shut up. I said I knew a short cut because she was soaking my clothes and the polis was looking for us. We had to cross over a railway line. We went down the embankment, rolling, falling. At the bottom we lay by the tracks. The trains were coming fast and I could feel the draught as they passed. I lay beside her and held her as they went by and said don't worry my darling I will soon have you in a hut and I'll put a bandage on your cut. She was shivering but it wasn't cold. There was a gap in the trains and we went over the tracks and up the embankment on the other side. We had to go through nettles and brambles and over a fence. Then we went into a garden and into the hut. Mandy fell on the floor and was still so I lay on the mattress which was there. In the morning I was hungry. Mandy was still there. She hadn't moved. There was dried blood all over her and her eyes were open. I said you daft wee bitch I didn't chib you that hard and went to get some food. On the way I phoned the polis and told them where she was. I got lifted 2 days later.

I know I done wrong by her but I'm brand new now and if I get released I will be OK.

                                                    James Purdue

Elka Willems closed the file and laid it back on the desk. 'I'm not impressed,' she said.

'Neither were the Parole Board,' said Sussock. 'Purdue was sentenced to ten years for the murder of Mandy McBride, aged nineteen years, a light sentence we thought and he served every minute. No remission for good behaviour for Jimmy the Rodent. The hall officers' report is in there somewhere and it would amount to a character assassination if it wasn't all true. Once he tried to chop off a screw's head with a metal tray. He got four years for serious assault but it fell within the span of his ten-year stretch so he didn't notice it.'

'So he came out twelve years ago and disappeared?'

'Yes, in a nutshell. Now he has re-appeared in connection with one girl who was murdered and another who has disappeared.'

'Presumed dead?'

'Presumed dead.'

'How are you going to set about finding him?'

'I was thinking of using Montgomerie's snout, Tuesday Noon by name.'

'He's talked of him to me.'

'Oh.'

'Yes,' said Elka Willems, leaning forward and smiling. 'When he asked me out.'

Sussock smiled. 'You never told me.'

'Didn't I? It must have slipped my mind.'

'Nothing slips your mind. What did you say to him?'

'I said I'd think about it.'

'What was his line?'

'Something along the lines of needing to get to know each other better because we work well together. He said he thought we had a natural affinity, a good rapport. I think he was implying that he thought we could touch souls, I think what he really meant was that we could touch each other's flesh.'

'Mind you, I like his line. I'll remember that.'

'And use it on who and when. You haven't got his panache, old Sussock. Tell me about Tuesday Noon.'

'He's a grimy, smelly old guy. Montgomerie meets up with him in a pub near the Round Toll up Woodside way. I'll leave a note asking Montgomerie to make contact with him. Purdue has a "loud" profile, Tuesday Noon will know where he is.'

The phone on his desk rang. Sussock reached forward

and picked it up, reaching for his pen and notepad as he did so.

Elka Willems watched his brow furrow. He wrote fully on his pad, but said little other than the occasional 'oh,' 'I see,' 'yes,' and eventually 'thank you.' He looked up at Elka Willems. 'Female corpse,' he said, 'partially clothed, evidence of violent attack. Found in a derelict tenement in Finnieston. Has been there for some time, a week, maybe more.'

'Any identification?'

'Toni Durham,' said Sussock.

It was Wednesday, 23.53 hours.

CHAPTER 7

Thursday, 00.30–06.45 hours

Violent attack, thought Sussock, was something of an understatement. Toni Durham hadn't been knifed so much as dissected. It was like stepping back twenty years for Sussock. Again here in this room were all the hallmarks of the work of James 'the Rodent' Purdue who didn't seem satisfied to take life, he wanted to destroy the life form as well. In this instance there was the additional unpleasantness of the putrefaction of a ten-day-old mutilated corpse.

Toni Durham's body had been found by a down-and-out. The man, reeking of alcohol and stale sweat, had spent the day walking round the town, rummaging in waste-bins, begging for ten pence for 'a cup of tea', eating what he could and at the very close of day, near to midnight, he returned to the den where he was 'skippering'. The man was still in his twenties but he was already immersed in the strange world of the down-and-out, the mental attitude of extreme detachment, wound up in his own thoughts, his own playacting, with a sense that all around him was a dream. Like all down-and-outs, he didn't like human company, even of other down-and-outs, because human company meant communicating and communicating meant leaving the comfort of the strange world and touching reality. 'Can you lend us ten pence for a cup of tea, sojer?' was the only exchange this man would offer, occasionally he might add 'ya bastard' as the 'soldier' swept by. So at the very end of the day he returned to his earlier home. He had not been there for the last three weeks: he'd been in the boiler room. The boiler room had been magic; he'd remember the boiler room for a long time. The door had been unlocked, then there was an inner door, a flight of steps, dry concrete floor and heat from the boiler. All the comforts of home. Then he had been discovered, ordered out. Tonight the door was securely locked so he returned to the derelict tenement in Finnieston. He went up the stair. He found other guys were still 'skippering' there, each with his own space in the empty rooms. There were wine bottles on the floor, super lager cans crushed in pent-up frustration. He had proceeded up the stair and found a bloody mess in his room, which was illuminated by a street lamp, he stood at the entrance to the room and swayed and tried to focus and he resented it, this mess. He resented it because this was other people's reality, it was the real world, and if he stayed he would have to leave the comfort of this fantasy world. He turned away from his room and shouted a warning and others came groping and fumbling up the stairs to the small room they never had occasion to visit and the word spread through the tenement. The down-and-outs packed up their rolls and plastic carrier bags. The first to leave were the younger ones who'd come down because of the needle, they were followed by the men who had just enough grasp of reality to remember that they were wanted on outstanding warrants, the rest followed because they knew that the body in the upper room meant the law, the law could

mean a night in the cells, a breach charge, a drying out spell,
it also meant Building Control and a new metal door on the
close. Either way the building was shot. No more skippering
here.

Phil Hamilton strolled down the street. It was a warm
night, quiet, not a lot had happened. Even the pubs had
turned out quietly. Then he noticed a figure step out of a
doorway, the figure carried a bundle and it slithered away
into the shadows and the darkness.

Then another followed.

Then another.

Then another and another and another.

Hamilton counted ten and then gave up counting but still
they came out and disappeared separately into the gloom,
all running from the same close. He quickened his pace. He
fancied he knew what had happened, a bottling, maybe one
had knifed another badly enough to cause a panic. He
reached the close mouth. The stench of sweat and stale
breath hung solidly in warm still air of the close. He went
into the close, torch in one hand, truncheon in the other,
one room at a time, one flat at a time, all were empty
but all revealed signs of recent human habitation, piles of
newsprint used as bedding, remains of fish supper carry-
outs, once he came across a down-and-out curled up in a
foetal position, snoring heavily and too comatose to have
been wakened by the commotion. Hamilton inched up the
stair, 'proceeding with caution'.

He smelled the body before he saw it. A sickly sweet,
nauseating smell. And the body, lying there, contorted and
stiff with rigor marks, her innards spilling out between her
ripped clothing, heaving with maggots, and her blood, dry
and black on the floor, on each wall. It was, thought
Hamilton, stepping back, gagging for breathable air, as if
she had been torn apart by a demon. He returned to the
room, snatched up the handbag lying close to the body,
opened it, a transcard, a few letters, a driver's licence, all

bearing the same name. He clutched his radio and radioed for assistance, a Code 41, believed to be one Toni Durham.

'She was torn apart,' said Sussock as the scene of crime officer pressed the camera flash. 'It's as though someone threw her to the wolves: she was more than murdered.'

'Has to be more than one assailant,' said Hamilton, still shaken by his discovery. The incident had leapt to the forefront of his 'worst things I ever saw' anecdotes and had done so by a length and a half.

'No, it hasn't,' said Sussock. 'This is the work of one man. I've been this way before.'

'He's a State Hospital number, then.'

'Certainly is. And if we'd have been able to prove that twenty years ago this lassie would still be alive.'

The camera flashed again. A constable, white-faced and agitated, approached Sussock. 'Police surgeon is here, sir.'

Sussock turned. 'Very good,' he said. 'Escort the gentle-man up the stair, please, laddie, advise him that the stair is dark and slippery.'

The duty police surgeon was Dr Chan. Sussock was pleased that the duty surgeon was Chan, he had always found Dr Chan to be polite, unhurried, but efficient, a calm presence, very professional, willing to put himself out, willing to stretch the remit of his job if he felt it would benefit the police and the public. He appeared in the doorway of the room in which lay the remains of Toni Durham. 'Oh my,' he said, 'oh my.'

In a house in the south side of the river a telephone rang. It was an old solid carbon-black phone which stood on a bedside cabinet, one of four phone extensions in the vast house, and it rang as it always did with a soft warbling purring note. A man reached a long sinewy arm out from the sheets, and extended it sleepily towards the phone, picking it up before it had rung three times. He spoke into the receiver. 'Reynolds,' he said.

Beside him his wife lay awake, stirred from her sleep by her husband speaking softly rather than by the ringing of the telephone. She lay still. She heard him replace the receiver and slide gently out of the bed, moving lightly for a tall man. She listened as he gently and quietly took clothing from the wardrobe and drawers so as to dress outside the room. He opened their bedroom door and shut it quietly behind him. Only then did Janet Reynolds open her eyes. She knew that her husband had done everything he could to prevent her sleep from being disturbed and she did not wish to disappoint him by letting him know that she had in fact woken. She looked at the luminous blue digits on the clock on the bedside cabinet. It was 02.14. She moaned, feeling a small measure of cause for complaint but largely managed to resist the feeling of having been cheated of sleep. She had retired early, at 10.00 p.m., had fallen asleep quickly and was now awake. She had still had four hours; more than enough for her. If her body didn't need sleep, it didn't need it, simple as that, and it was something she no longer felt unsettled about. Once it had occurred to her, as it did in a momentous flash of realization while she was shopping one day, years ago, that insomnia meant she was getting many more active waking hours in her lifespan of three score and ten than the average person, once she had accepted the notion that her insomnia effectively lengthened her life, if not in terms of years yet in terms of measurable periods of consciousness, then it became a privilege to be an insomniac. It was a stroke of good fortune. She was, she told herself, a woman who had everything, a wonderful, successful husband, two beautiful children, a fabulous house and five hours in each twenty-four hours that were hers and hers alone to do with as she pleased. It was, she convinced herself, really a question of attitude. Once she had stopped seeing herself as weird or as being some kind of freak just because she didn't sleep nights, once she had stopped lying in the darkness turning, tossing, trying to sleep, once she had stopped trying to knock herself out with sleeping pills or alcohol and sometimes in dangerous desperation both sleeping pills and alcohol combined, once she realized she could make her insomnia work for her, then from that point her whole life changed. She became more confident, she began to like herself, she went out more and eventually met a man who became her husband and now, in her late thirties, because of the extra five hours a day, not only was she running a home and successfully raising her children, but she had studied for a higher degree at Glasgow University, had learned three foreign languages and had devoured an enormous amount of literature.

She lay on her back looking at the ceiling, just able to make out the ornamental plasterwork in the gloom. She listened to her husband descend the stair, hiss 'Quiet!' as Gustav the St Bernard barked as he entered the kitchen. Sounds, she had noticed, tend to carry at night, even in such a huge house as hers. She heard the gentle 'clink' of a teaspoon stirring in a mug as her husband made himself a cup of instant coffee which she knew he would be drinking with the lump of cheese he would be eating. 'Never,' Dr Reynolds had impressed on his family, 'never go out without something in your stomach. Your body is an engine. It needs fuel. Food and drink is your body's fuel. In winter you keep the cold out with food. In summer keep the heat out with hot, not cold, drink, hot tea is more cooling on a summer's day than chilled lemon juice, and never drink alcohol if you feel dehydrated.' And not being the hypocrite in any aspect of his life, she knew that her husband would not leave the house at this hour without a fresh intake of both fluid and food, no matter how urgently the police required his presence. She lay in bed and heard the front door open and shut, the Volvo start up and the whine of the reverse gear as it was backed down the drive and on to the road. She listened as he drove away, first, second, third, then top gear and was again astounded for how long in a still night she could hear her husband's car. Finally it faded from her hearing. She switched on the light, dressed, went downstairs. She let Gustav out into the rear garden, percolated some coffee and then curled up in her husband's favourite chair with holiday brochures and planned her family's winter break: sun or snow? Life's all right, really.

Reynolds took the Clydeside Expressway exit from the Kingston Bridge, pulled over, consulted his copy of the street atlas and drove into Finnieston, turning right and left down dark streets until he came across a scene of police activity.

Minutes later Reynolds looked on horrified as Sussock played the beam of a torch over the mutilated corpse and around the room, the blood on the floor and the walls, the ceiling, good God in heaven there was even blood on the ceiling. 'How many attacked her?' he asked.

'Just one, sir,' said Sussock, switching off his torch. 'Just one.' He spoke softly, calmly yet his voice carried as clear as a tolling bell on a still night. 'I met him once.'

'Well, I can't do anything here. I'll have the body removed to the mortuary. I'll take a few maggots as well.'

'Maggots, sir?'

'Maggots, Sergeant. They'll help me determine the time of death.'

'I see.'

'One other thing, Sergeant, I couldn't help noticing syringes lying in some of the rooms, the building is probably moving with the AIDS virus. You'd better warn your men to be careful if touching anything sharp, treat syringes, broken bottles, torn cans, old razors, etcetera with the utmost respect.'

'I'll pass the word, sir. Thank you.'

*

The harsh ringing of the phone woke Elliot Bothwell. He rolled over, twisted, curled up into a ball but the phone wouldn't stop ringing. Eventually he extended a flabby arm and groped for the phone and succeeded in knocking it on to the floor. He searched the floor, feeling with his hand, located the cord and pulled the receiver towards him, taking it deep into the recesses of the sheets. 'Yes,' he said. Then: 'OK, I'll be right there.'

He pushed the sheets back, it being high summer he needed no other bedding, and wiped the sleep from his eyes. He rolled out of bed, washed and returned to his room to dress.

His mother called from her room, 'Elliot, Elliot . . . that you?'

'Yes, Mother,' he said automatically while dressing. He was thirty-six years old, awkward in movement, and bespectacled. He felt gauche in every waking moment and wanted to be married. He wanted that very badly. He opened the curtains and looked out on to the backs, grey and shadowy, the cats creating dark mounds which moved along the walls and were still again. He left the flat, pulling the heavy dark-stained door behind him, went down the common stair still reeking with disinfectant from the previous day's wash, and went out into the street. A milk-float rattled past. Dawn was rising in Queen's Park. Elliot Bothwell drove to Finnieston in his beat-up Fiat. By the time he arrived the body had been removed and most of the cops had left. Just two officers remained, one at the entrance of the close, one at the top of the stair outside the locus of the offence.

'It's all yours,' said the cop at the top of the stair, 'and welcome to it.'

'Bad?' Bothwell shuffled through the doorway, carrying his case.

'Bad enough, friend,' said the cop. 'And I've to tell you to be careful of any sharp edges, the doctor said the building is probably alive with AIDS.'

Bothwell muttered a 'thanks for the warning' and stepped into the room, where the scene of crime officer had left lamps burning to assist Bothwell's work. He found that the floorboards, the walls and even the ceiling were stained with a dark brown, almost black substance. He was surprised that the human body could hold so much blood and that it could be spread so liberally. It was as if a bucket of blood had been sloshed about the room. And the maggots didn't help, fat bloated maggots, crawling about the floor, chewing on the dried blood. He saw that one corner of the room seemed to have been undefiled by blood and bits of gore. He crossed to it and laid his case down. The room was bare of furnishings, no flat surface at all save for the floor and walls, so he decided, dust for prints on the bottles and cans, photograph the fingerprints on the wall, photograph the footprints and fingerprints on the floor, in fact there's one I can see it from here, get the lamp down low, cast a long shadow . . .

To the constable who stood at the entrance of the flat Elliot Bothwell presented a strange figure, short, overweight, hurriedly dressed, his tie trapping one side of his shirt collar, he 'bumbled' about the room, occasionally muttering, comical in an unkind sort of way. If Bothwell was aware of the constable looking at him and concealing mirth he was unconcerned by it. He just got on with his job: looking for fingerprints in dried blood in derelict houses at 3.30 in the morning. It certainly wasn't everybody's idea of easy money but it was better than the alternative, that being the job he had previously held as a chemistry assistant in a secondary school. Year in, year out, he mixed the same calm chemicals for a class of adolescents and saw no result except the steady greying of the chemistry teacher's hair. Then he noticed a post advertised in the Regional Council internal vacancy bulletin: a forensic assistant's post with the Strathclyde Police, attached to P Division at Charing Cross, was vacant. He applied, got the job, and never looked back. Now no

jobs were ever the same. So he still wasn't paid much but
he saw life in all its rawness.

An hour and a half after Elliot Bothwell had entered the
room in the derelict tenement he stood and glanced about
him, turning through three hundred and sixty degrees. Done
that, that surface, that surface, photographed that, that,
that and that. Got that there on the wall, that on the
floor, that by the door handle. It was the scene of crime
officer's responsibility to record the locus, the body in situ,
the overview, before and after the removal of the body. It
was his job as forensic assistant to record the details, the
fingerprints, the footprints, the details on which a successful
prosecution often depends. It was not his job to identify
them, it was his job to lift them, record them, mount them
and then pass them on to the next square in the procedural
diagram. He was keenly aware that a successful identification of a latent depended on patience and diligence on his
part. A smudged lifting, an unswept surface, could mean
the grinding to a halt of the police machine, it could mean
a killer walking or an innocent man thrown in the slammer.
Here, here in this death room, this sweetly smelling, bare-
floorboarded, chipped plaster-walled box, where a young
woman's blood had been spilled, here was where he had to
exercise his responsibility, just him and him alone. His was
a responsibility he found awesome and the more he thought
about it, the more awesome it became.

He tried not to think about it, he just did his job as
diligently and methodically as he could. Satisfied that he
had diligently and methodically recorded and lifted all
evidence there was to record and lift, he knelt down, closed
his plastic case and snapped the clasps shut. He'd been able
to lift prints from bottles and cans, doubtless belonging to
the down-and-out whose home this had been, prints on the
wall which might be his too, but the prints in the blood
including whole palm prints had to be the prints of the
deceased or of the killer. These he recorded with special

care. The killer or the killers? Judging by the amount and extent of dark brown substance dried to the floor and the walls and the ceiling, Bothwell felt it would be reasonable to assume the killers in this case to have been a pack of hunting dogs. He'd shot off three rolls of film and lifted an additional six latents with iron filings, spreading the filings over the prints, sweeping them with a squirrel-hair brush and revealing an impression of the fingerprint by dint of those filings which adhered to it. This he transferred on to a roll of adhesive paper. He glanced out of the grimy window. It was getting light with just a few high white clouds to be seen. It would soon be another hot dry day in a hot dry summer. Pretty soon the room would be black with flies.

Time to go, Elliot.

'Well, it was a frenzied attack.' Reynolds had switched off the microphone and spoke directly to Ray Sussock. The two men were alone in the room, thankfully, from Sussock's point of view, free of the presence of the mortuary assistant. On this occasion Reynolds conducted the post mortem without assistance. Reynolds leaned over the tattered and twisted remnants of Toni Durham's body, resting both hands on the 'lip' of the stainless steel table. 'At a conservative estimate I'd say she sustained seventy to eighty stab wounds.'

'A conservative estimate?' Sussock echoed Reynolds's words. The pathologist nodded. 'Could be over one hundred in fact, anything from a superficial scratch to deep penetration, particularly around her intestines, she looks as though she's been gutted. Butchered like an animal, probably after all the fight had been spilled from her and she lay dying. You can never get used to this, can you?'

'Never.' Sussock meant it. Even with thirty years at the coal face of police work, and having seen Jimmy 'the Rodent' Purdue's handiwork before, he still found the remains of Toni Durham a distressing spectacle.

'I suppose that when you get used to it, then that's the time to give up and breed sheepdogs for a living. Cause of death, you name it, major trauma, multiple lacerations causing massive if not near-total loss of blood, shock, she died the death of one thousand cuts. If you want the *coup de grâce* it could be the puncture of the aorta but that wound could have been sustained after death, there's no way of telling. In layman's terms she was ripped open. That's the long and the short of it.'

'The murder weapon, sir?'

'Well, a knife, narrow five, six-inch blade, one sharp edge, a strong blade because there's evidence of a ripping motion. Some of the wounds give the impression of her having been mauled by a clawed creature.'

'Time of death, sir?'

Reynolds shrugged. 'Ten days perhaps, the decay is well advanced as one would expect from the hot airless room in which she was found. I've collected some maggots, there's a method I can use to determine the probable time of death from those wee beasties, but I would think that their growth would indicate putrefaction of seven days, which would indicate death some two or three days prior to that.'

'I see, sir.'

'Have you made any identification,' Reynolds asked. 'I mean, you're not going to ask the next of kin to identify the body in this condition?'

'I really haven't thought so far ahead,' Sussock conceded. 'Mind you, the relatives may wish to view the body, the head at least. They have the right.'

'I'm aware of that. I could tidy her face up, shampoo the blood from her hair, the nose and cheekbones have been broken. I can make her clean but I can't hide the damage. Fortunately they won't want to see the rest of her body. I can kill the smell for long enough with alcohol. That's if they want to see the body, or if it's necessary for them to do so. I would have thought that dental records or fingerprinting would be a more appropriate form of verifying her identity.'

'I think you're right, sir,' said Sussock. 'I think you're right.'

He forced himself to look at the corpse, carved open in one hundred places, stiff and rigid, bloated, the intestines hanging out. God in heaven, she was a mess.

Sussock drove across the city from the GRI to P Division Police Station at Charing Cross. Dawn had broken, an hour to go before rush hour began but already the sky was high and blue. Milk roundsmen whistling in shirtsleeves dropped cartons of milk at the doorways of offices and shops, newspaper vans drove to deserted streets delivering early editions to vendors who waited at their street-corner pitches. He drove along Bath Street, up and over the hump, solid buildings on either side of him, and into the car park at the rear of the police station. He signed in, checked his pigeonhole, went up to the CID corridor to his office and hung his hat on the hat-stand. He left his office and went to where Abernethy sat alone at a desk, his being the only occupied desk in a room of four desks. Abernethy was working a double shift at short notice.

Abernethy was sifting through the contents of Toni Durham's handbag, just as hours earlier Donoghue had sifted through the contents of Stephanie Craigellachie's handbag.

'Anything of interest?' asked Sussock. He felt tired. The graveyard shift was no type of work for a man of his years, and as always the last few hours of the shift were the longest as the building seemed to quieten, to enter a lull, as the clocks ticked and dragged towards 7.00 a.m.

'A key ring, Building Society passbook, nice comfortable balance there.'

'Oh?'

Abernethy handed Sussock the passbook and Sussock

said, 'Wow!' Toni Durham had enough money to buy three or four 'desirable' west end properties outright and still have money left over to furnish each.

'Be interesting to pin down the source of that income, Sarge, but I reckon it has something to do with her being a Ms Fix-it.'

Abernethy took the passbook as Sussock handed it to him.

'Be very interesting,' said Sussock. then: 'You're looking pale, son.'

'Didn't want it to show.' Abernethy patted a folder which also lay on his desk. 'Photographs sent up by the scene of crime officer, Sarge. Shows Toni Durham, or what's left of her. I've never seen anything like it.'

'I'm afraid I have, some years before, about the time that you would be running round in short trousers, and I saw Toni Durham's body at the pathology lab just now. It's just like the photograph except it's three-dimensional, five and a half feet long, and it smells.'

'Smells? Of blood?'

'Of dried blood, of human gases and it smelled of death, despite being washed down with alcohol. Did you know that death has a smell, son?'

Abernethy confessed that he did not.

'You've seen a dead body, though?'

'Yes, Sarge, every cop has, a visit to a mortuary is part of basic training. A car smash I attended, two car accidents in fact, some badly damaged human beings in there, but even the car smashes were not as bloody as this.' He patted the envelope.

'But you've never smelled death. The mortuary is sanitized, the car smash victims were just too new. Death smells like dried leaves but it has a sweet property among the mustiness, it's difficult to describe but once you've smelled it you'll never forget it and you'll always recognize it again, and all human beings smell the same at their death, young, old, rich, poor, man, woman, they all leave the same legacy. The smell was the last thing Toni Durham left behind her and if she was running with Jimmy Purdue and had accumulated this sort of money then she will have left little else of note behind her.'

'You know Jimmy "the Rodent" Purdue?'

'Yes. It's what I meant a minute ago when I said I'd seen victims as messy as Miss Durham while you were in short trousers. Toni Durham's body has all the hallmarks of an attack by Purdue. I should know, I've seen his handiwork before. I helped put him away when I was a fresh cop. He got ten years and I said then that he was a State Hospital number and if we can pin this murder on him then he will definitely be a Carstairs inmate. I'm a spit short of my pension and I'll bet it, even money, that he did this. I mean, if anyone is criminally insane, it's Jimmy "the Rodent" Purdue. I'm going to start looking for him; being a known associate of the deceased is a good enough reason to start.'

'Oh, you've got more than that, Sarge.' Abernethy tapped the phone which stood on his desk. 'While you were at the pathology lab attending the post mortem, criminal records phoned with information. They've identified one set of prints which Elliot Bothwell lifted from the locus of the offence as belonging to your man Purdue.'

Sussock smiled. 'That's good enough for me.'

'It'll be even better when I tell you where one of Purdue's many latents was found: on the wall in Toni Durham's blood. The blood has been identified as the same blood group as the deceased's and the latent is apparently so deeply indented in the blood that he had to have been there when the blood was still tacky, he was there during the assault, that's the point that Forensic makes, passed on to us through criminal records. It's not on a bloodless piece of plaster so he can't say he was there before the assault, it wasn't left on dried blood so he can't argue he was there after the assault took place. It's a clear left thumbprint, apparently pushed deep into wet blood. It means he was there during the assault.'

Sussock grunted. 'He's nailed. With that alone he's nailed.'

'All we need to do is find him.'

'We'll just need to be methodical. The city's full of rat holes and he'll be in one of them. I reckon the first post of call is Toni Durham's flat. We have a set of house keys and an address in the Building Society book. Grab your coat, this will kill the shift for us.'

Abernethy grabbed his coat, amazed at the sudden trans-formation in Sussock. The man who had shuffled up to his desk ten minutes ago was now like a terrier with a bone.

Toni Durham's flat was a ground-floor five apartment in a prestigious street close to Great Western Road, opposite the Botanical Gardens. There was a small, neatly tended front garden and a gravel pathway leading up the side of the building to the front door. The curtains inside the property were open. Sussock rang the doorbell. As he listened to the bell chime inside the house he noticed just one name on the door: Durham. He said, 'She doesn't share with anybody.'

'So what does she do with all this space?' Abernethy glanced along the length of the side of the property.

An orange bus hurried down Great Western Road towards the traffic lights at the top of Byres Road. A milk-float rattled up the incline towards the Hyndland turn-off. The sun was already well over the rooftops, it was a warm, clean morning, promising a hot, hot day.

'Nobody at home,' said Sussock, and took the bunch of keys which had been found in Toni Durham's handbag from his jacket pocket.

Toni Durham did not just live in the five apartment flat, according to a rates demand issued the previous April and still lying on the hall table, she was the householder. Not only was she the householder, but she was a householder who could apparently afford to decorate the property in a manner which afforded her every indulgence. She favoured light pastel shades and soft furnishings, deep pile carpets, pictured wallpaper, Chinese lantern lampshades. Fronds of pampas spraying from a large cream-coloured urn, a light brown, old-fashioned style, but very modern telephone. Very chic, very feminine. The sun streamed in through the tall, tall windows picking out flecks of dust in the air.

'Dead,' said Sussock.

'Sarge?'

'This house, it's dead. It's not lived in. It's like something out of the Ideal Homes Exhibition.' Sussock had experienced a momentary pang of envy as he entered Toni Durham's flat, but after only a few minutes inside he could safely say he would prefer, vastly prefer, to spend time in his cramped, noisy bedsitter. The little things out of place made it lived in. 'Mind you, I'd like to know where little Miss Durham got the money to buy this property and furnish it like this. Just look at the hi-fi she has.'

'And a telephone-answering machine, I mean, she just had to have . . .' Abernethy's voice failed as both he and Sussock realized the significance of the green flashing light on the answering machine.

Sussock strode across the carpet and pressed the 'message' button on the machine. The cops stood, listening, to the accumulated recordings.

'Hello, Toni, this is Mother . . .'

'She'll need to be told,' grunted Sussock.

'. . . we were wondering if you're coming round this Sunday. You know that we'd like to see you. Give us a call, hen. 'Bye.'

The machine gave a lood, piercing 'beep'.

'The garage here, Miss Durham. Just to let you know your car's sorted. You can collect it any time.'

beep

'Gary at the travel agent's, we've got all the details you

required for your Canada trip . . . and details of the side trips you wanted to make . . . er . . . you'll need a visa if you want to visit the States . . . we can fix that for you if you'd like to ring me back. Right, that's me. 'Bye.'

beep

'Aye, you and your fancy wee toys, hen . . .

'Purdue,' Sussock hissed. 'I'd recognize that voice anywhere. Hard as concrete. Cold as ice.'

'. . . see, we've got a wee problem with that Craigellachie girl. The one you brought round and said was OK. She's talking. And she's lifted a ton of smack. We need to sort it out. Meet me tonight, junction at Minerva Street and Argyle Street. Tonight. Just be there.'

That's close to where she was found,' said Sussock. 'He must have taken her to the derelict building and filled her in.'

'Dates these messages,' said Abernethy. 'They're up to ten days old at the beginning.'

beep

'It's Mum again, pet. Just giving you a ring.'

beep

'The garage again, Miss Durham. Called you two days ago and left a message on your machine. Can you collect your car, please? It's all sorted. Thanks.'

beep

'Sonia from the parlour. Just wondering if you'd fancy a drink and a blether? Phone me. 'Bye.'

beep

'Toni, it's Stephanie . . .'

Abernethy and Sussock glanced at each other.

'. . . see, that guy with the Mercedes, he pulled me off the street, took me to a house . . . he gave me a doing, Toni . . . I need to see you . . . the guy's mad . . . see his eyes, just burning into me . . . please contact me at my flat . . . please.'

So, thought Sussock, that's what Stephanie Craigellachie

sounded like, a thin high-pitched voice. But she was frightened. His voice would be thin and high-pitched if he was frightened.

beep

'Toni, Stephanie again. I phoned this morning . . . will you call round, or maybe contact me on the street, you know where my pitch is, see, that guy Purdue, he said he's going to find you, take care, he'll likely give you a good tanking as well. I'm scared, look after yourself, what's happening, Toni? That's my ten pence . . .'

beep

'The garage, Miss Durham. If you don't collect your car I'll have to take it off the premises and leave it in the street. I haven't the room to keep it.'

beep

'Gary at the travel agent's. If you'd like to call and see me, Miss Durham, I have all the details of your Canada trip.'

beep

'It's Stephanie. You going to contact me? I'm scared. I'm told that that guy Purdue's looking for me. So I daren't go on the street for a while, even if the other girls keep the edge for me, they've got work to do, can't keep a lookout all the time, I'll need more smack soon, that load you gave me is running low . . . it's good stuff, where did you get it . . . can you get some more? Please . . .'

beep

'This is your father. Listen, I'm not bothered if I don't see you again, you wee bitch, you should get married and have kids like your sisters, that would sort you out, we don't know what you're doing, never see you from one month to the next, then you drop in with your fancy clothes and your flash motor. Just call your mother, it's been three weeks now, she's getting worried, and she'll no give me peace because she's fretting about you. I was too soft with you. I let you away with too much because you were the youngest.

That was my mistake. Phone her, preferably when I'm at work.'

beep

'The garage. I'm having to leave your car on the street as from tonight, Miss Durham.'

beep

'Toni, it's Stephanie. They're saying Purdue's after me because I half-inched his smack. Toni, that bag of smack you gave me, it was his, wasn't it, you bitch, you cow. You lifted it from him and gave it to me. He thinks I nicked it. He's going to kill me now because of you and I've got nowhere to hide. It's almost shot now, then I'll have to go back on the street to get more money . . . and they're saying I've been shouting my mouth off about what you and Purdue do in your basement . . .'

The cops looked at each other.

' . . .Toni, I never said nothing to nobody. You've done for me, you cow. You've stitched me up proper. What for? I done nothing to you. If I get the chance I'm going to tell him, but he'll not listen . . . he's mad.'

beep

'This is your father. Call your mother, you slag.'

beep

'Toni, that's the smack shot. I'm having to go on to the street again. Don't know why I'm telling you. Just tell Purdue it wasn't me that stole his smack.'

beep

'It's Mum. Call me, love. Dad said he phoned. I know what he can be like, don't take it personal. He'll not be home till the back of six each weekday, call me any time before five and we can have a blether. I don't want to go on at you, dear, but a quick hello wouldn't take up too much of your time. I mean, it's been a good few weeks now and you could be lying dead somewhere . . . oh, I shouldn't say things like that. Just give me a ring. 'Bye.'

beep

'Gary at the travel shop . . . er, just to say you'll need to pay up the balance of your trip in the next two weeks, otherwise we'll have to let the tickets go. Just call in if you're passing. If I'm not in tell anyone that they're in my desk . . . that's Gary's desk. 'Bye.'

beep

'Toni, it's Stephanie . . . are you all right? One of the girls on the street, . . . no, it was Sonia who works the parlour, said that guy Purdue pulled her last night, he was steaming drunk, said he'd filled you in . . . Toni, you OK? He said he was looking for me too. I'm scared. I can't earn money by hanging in the shadows . . . and I need a fix, I'm getting strung out. I'm getting bad, that stuff you gave me was good stuff, I'm going to be real bad this time if I don't get another fix. I'll need to go on the street tonight, earn a big wad, anything they want me to do tonight, but Purdue's going to cool me if I go out, I'll try and wait till it's dark, work the casinos . . . Toni, I won't tell him nothing if you can get me some horse. I didn't mean what I said when I said I'd shop you to Purdue. He can give me all the doings he wants if you can let me have more of that horse. I'll be on the street tonight, opposite the bank near the building site. Please, Toni.'

beep

'Toni, it's Sonia, Sonia from the parlour, I'd have called earlier but I couldn't get away. Listen, I ran into that guy Purdue, blitzed out of his mind. He was legless, I mean moroculous, he hadn't even got half a brain left. He said he'd done you in and was looking for that girl Craigellachie, was she that girl you brought here, Toni? Jesus, woman, she's just a kid, what have you got her mixed up in, Toni? Pulling schoolgirls for your films now, this'll need some talking about, even people like me have a code of honour. I've got people I can call on to carve you if you deserve it. Just remember that.'

beep

The tape rewound, back to the beginning. Sussock took the cassette from the machine and slipped it into his jacket pocket. 'Interesting reference to the basement,' he said.

'Intriguing,' said Abernethy.

The entrance to the basement eluded the cops until they noticed that an area of floor close to the kitchen sounded hollow when walked on. It sounded even hollower when Sussock stamped his foot on the area. They lifted the carpet and revealed a trapdoor.

The basement they found ran the whole length and breadth of the house with an identical configuration of rooms, effectively doubling the floor area of the property. The ceiling was low, only about eight feet above the floor, but affording sufficient room for both cops to be able to walk upright. The basement had been re-floored and the walls had been plastered smoothly and painted white. Lighting had been installed and additional powerful lamps stood on chrome poles in each of the doorless 'rooms'. Two of the rooms had double beds, both with crumpled sheets, another had a settee and a table, another room seemed to have been made into a gymnasium with benches and wall bars. A wooden chest contained items of female clothing fashioned out of leather and PVC. In the smallest room cameras were stored and wall racks contained row upon row of blank video tapes still in the manufacturer's Cellophane wrapping. Others, of equal number, had been used and were stocked in date order.

'Imagine,' said Sussock. 'Movie moguls beavering away in fair Glasgow town and we never knew about it.'

'Amazing,' said Abernethy.

The man lay in bed next to his heavy wife. He was awake, watching the early morning sun stream in through the net curtains of their bedroom. Dawn had come to Newton Mearns.

She even whistled in her sleep. He thought she must

inhabit such a perfect world, never seeing anything of life for what it was. Just pretty things.

There was an awful loneliness in his life and he wondered if he went to town in the evening then perhaps this time he'd see Stephanie. Perhaps she'd been ill for a few days. That would explain it.

CHAPTER 8

Thursday, 08.45–12.17 hours

Donoghue reached forward and replenished his cup from the silver-plated coffee jar which stood on his desk. The coffee at the beginning of the working day was part of his morning routine; it eased, as he was fond of saying, the mechanics of the shift hand-over. He raised the pot. 'Ray?'

Sussock sat forward in his chair, extended his hand, holding his own mug while Donoghue refilled it. 'Thank you, sir,' he said. He was bleary-eyed. Donoghue was fresh-faced and had already taken his jacket off, but had declined to loosen the knot of his tie. Sussock sat in his baggy, sack-like sports jacket and cradled his mug of coffee in both hands. Ordinarily he found the shift hand-overs tedious especially if he was going off duty and Donoghue, coming on duty, was keen to 'kick around' points of trivia. On this occasion, though, he had something to contribute. He had not been idle, he had made good progress.

'Odd, isn't it?' Donoghue reclined in his chair and glanced out of the window at the morning sun glinting on the glass and concrete buildings of the city's central business district. He thought suddenly that in eight hours' time the city's working girls would be standing underneath those buildings.

'Sir?' Sussock looked at Donoghue. 'Odd, sir?'

Donoghue nodded towards the cassette player on his

desk. 'The voices, the voices of dead people. Toni Durham
had been dead for ten days by the time Stephanie Craigellachie made her last call.'

'It's an odd sensation,' agreed Sussock. 'Myself, I was
struck by the emptiness of Toni Durham's life. Even ten
days after he was murdered no one, not even her parents or
sisters, thought she might be dead. It gives some indication
of the length of time they went without seeing each other, I
mean given that they live in the same city. Other than her
family, the only people to phone her in those ten days were
the garage, the travel agent, the man who was to kill her
and somebody called Sonia. And of course the desperate
and frightened Stephanie Craigellachie. Imagine all that
wealth and a cavernous flat in Westbourne Gardens and no
one to enjoy it with.'

'You ran the video tapes through?'

'Not all of them, sir, just a random sample. Just what
you'd expect: ham-acted, hard-core pornography. We'll
have to sit through all of them—'

'We'll sit through none of them,' Donoghue said sharply.
'I intend to hand the whole cache over to the Vice Squad.
I have an appointment with Vice later today, I'll let them
know what's coming their way. We'll let them know what
and who we're interested in and hopefully they'll edit it out
and pass it back to us.'

'Well, that's a relief,' said Sussock. 'There must be over
a thousand hours of the stuff.'

'It's where they go when they get too old to work the
street.' Donoghue opened the file that Sussock had laid
on his desk, the contents of which spoke of a productive
graveyard shift. Sussock saw Donoghue wince as he took
out the photograph of Toni Durham's corpse. Donoghue
looked at the photograph, once, briefly. It was enough. 'Did
you see her in the video tapes?'

Sussock shook his head. 'No, but we did see Stephanie
Craigellachie and another girl. Just by chance, I was fast-

forwarding and stopping at random and found a scene, some scene, there they both were together deshabille, on the same bed with a handsome toyboy and giving him one hell of a good time.'

'Good for him,' said Donoghue drily. 'So what's to be done? A warrant for the arrest of Jimmy "the Rodent" Purdue would be a good start. So you know him from way back, Ray?'

'From way back indeed, sir. He's one of those overgrown neds that surfaces from time to time, no real style, no skills, no organization. Just downright vicious. Keep him humoured and he might, just might, not chib you. Rattle his cage and you're dead. Toni Durham's death has all the hallmarks of Purdue's style and it doesn't surprise me in the slightest that Elliot Bothwell found Purdue's paw prints in his victim's blood. He's a messy worker, Purdue, I mean. About twenty years ago—well, close on—he went down for the murder of a lassie, came out after ten years and disappeared. I assumed that he had burnt out or "matured", which I believe are the official terms given to psychopaths who no longer kill or maim without evident cause. Obviously I was wrong.'

'Well, so it seems, Ray. He seems to have submerged himself into Glasgow's other film industry and has done very well by all accounts, the Mercedes and stylish clothes, I mean. Did he always have this passion for females?'

'Apparently.' Sussock shifted in his seat. 'I heard a story from when he was wee, about ten years old, he had his sister of thirteen on the ground, he had a blade at her throat and was pawing her with his free hand. His sister was rigid with fear, and he was discovered by his mother who quite literally had to knock him out with a length of timber before he'd let go. They took him unconscious to the Vicky, they used to stay next to the Victoria Infirmary, and told the staff he'd fallen downstairs. He was kept in for observation but woke up, demanded his clothes and swaggered out of the hospital as though nothing had happened. He wasn't out for revenge or anything, he just wanted a blade for one hand and a lassie for the other. The story goes that the kids on the south side all knew him, especially the girls; there would always be one of them not allowed to join in the fun, that one had to stand and keep the edge for Jimmy Purdue. He could clear a park or play area in fifteen seconds just by being seen walking towards it. In the end he resorted to creeping up on his victims commando-style, then rushing out of the bushes or from round the corner or whatever, grabbing his victim and paw, paw, paw. Anybody that tried to interfere would get ripped with his blade.'

'I think I've heard tales of him.' Donoghue sipped his coffee. 'Part of the rich folklore of our city.'

'You would have done, sir,' Sussock said. Donoghue noticed a hardness entering Sussock's voice. 'He grew up to get away with murder. Literally. And he did so, times without number. There were knifings a-plenty south of the water that were all down to him, we knew that, but see getting a witness to testify? Impossible. Worse than that, there was often some poor sucker who'd be willing to take the rap. God knows what Jimmy Purdue had to hold over them but not a few times some big softy said, 'Yes, I did it,' when we knew fine well it was Purdue's doing. He's a pure animal. I said it before and I'll say it again. He's a State Hospital number. He needs a single to Carstairs Junction.'

'Certainly sounds like it.' Donoghue reached for his pipe and spent what for Sussock was an annoyingly long time lighting it. It was Donoghue's first pipe of the day and Sussock knew that from this point on the Detective-Inspector would be surrounded with a haze of blue tobacco smoke. 'So,' said Donoghue sucking and blowing, 'Jimmy "the Rodent" Purdue, public enemy number one, where is he?'

Sussock made a don't-ask-me gesture.

Donoghue smiled. 'Where do we begin to look for him? What are his haunts, his natural habitat?'

'Again, I don't really know, sir,' said the older cop, and once again Donoghue noticed just how tired Ray Sussock was looking these days. 'If you'd have asked me that twenty years ago when he went down for murder, I'd have said any one of three bars in the Saltmarket, tough, seedy bars, closed up now, wine and spirit bars, strictly men only, the sort of places where blood was left lying if it didn't come off with the first swipe of the mop. But as you said, he seems to have come up in the world and seems to have grown to like money. Before he went down he just lusted after women and power, so long as he had enough doh-ray-me for a night's bevvying then he was happy, he could sink a good bucket, mind you, so one night on the bevvy was a costly operation, but nevertheless power, not money, was his vice. Today who knows?'

'All right. Let's look at it from another angle. Where does he fit in with Toni Durham and Stephanie Craigellachie? What was the connection between those girls?'

'Well, going by their respective lifestyles, Abernethy's report, the content of the recorded phone calls, I'd say that Toni Durham was up to her oxters in porno movies and heroin, I'd say that she stole heroin from Purdue, I mean a good lump of it and told Purdue that Stephanie Craigellachie nicked it. Maybe she had a motive, maybe it was just pure spite.'

Donoghue nodded in approval.

Sussock continued. 'I'd say that Toni Durham lured Stephanie Craigellachie into the movies with the promise of easy money and lots of smack. Stephanie started talking, she might have had a bit of a loose tongue. So Purdue filled in Toni Durham for bringing a nuisance into the company, then he went looking for the nuisance, who had gone to ground until she had filled herself with the heroin that Toni Durham had given her.'

'He must have known that sooner or later she would have to come back to the street, sooner or later she'd get strung out and need money for another fix.' Donoghue tapped black ash from his pipe into the huge ashtray which stood on his desk. 'The fact that he killed Toni Durham is significant, given her lifestyle. What I mean is that he was not in any way in her pay, or dependent on her, and since she was comfortably off, he must be equally so. It's my guess that Purdue and Toni Durham were business partners, until Purdue saw fit to make his business partner a permanently sleeping partner.'

'And then he went looking for Stephanie Craigellachie with the same murderous intent. She gets it in the neck, literally, but he doesn't pull her skin from bone as he would normally have done, he seems to have been disturbed. He even left the knife sticking in her throat.'

'Be handy if we could find out who disturbed him,' said Donoghue. 'Make a very handy witness. Anyway, there's a lot for the day shift to worry away at. I've a meeting with Chief Superintendent Findlater later this morning to apprise him of progress to date, so let's kick it about. What's to be done?'

'Well, we have to find Jimmy "the Rodent' Purdue," said Sussock, feeling too tired to kick anything about.

'Yes.' Donoghue nodded. 'We'll certainly have to make that our number one priority. I'll get a warrant for his arrest sworn as soon as I can. You have no idea of where we can start looking, Ray?'

'He'll be known to the underworld,' Sussock ventured. 'We can ask questions.'

'Montgomerie's got a useful snout, Wednesday Lunchtime . . .'

'Tuesday Noon.'

'Tuesday Noon,' Donoghue repeated. 'Montgomerie's on day shift today. He'll be at his desk at the moment so I'll see him immediately after this discussion. Now I don't want to let go of this character Dino—you remember he has the dubious accolade of having his name tattooed on Stephanie Craigellachie's most private or private parts? I don't want to chase a red herring, but I still feel that Dino is a stone worth turning over.'

'We'll also have to inform Toni Durham's next of kin.'

Donoghue nodded. 'I was forgetting that, Ray, thank you.' He scribbled on his pad. 'At least we're sure of her identification, so we can spare them the ordeal of having to view the body. Never easy for anyone, but in this case it's not an experience to be chased.'

'Certainly isn't,' said Sussock, rising from his seat and placing his mug on Donoghue's desk. He sensed the 'kicking about' to be over, having been thankfully brief.

Donoghue strode down the corridor to the detective-constable's room. Montgomerie was there, clean cut and well dressed, sitting at his desk, browsing through the day's edition of the *Glasgow Herald*.

'No work to do, Montgomerie?' said Donoghue.

Montgomerie shut the newspaper and slammed it into his in-tray. 'Just about to start, sir.'

'Good. Well, before you do whatever you are going to do, I'd like you to hunt down your informant, Tuesday Noon.'

'Oh?'

'Yes. We're anxious to trace a felon by the name of Jimmy "the Rodent" Purdue.'

Montgomerie glanced questioningly at Donoghue. 'That name rings bells,' he said. 'Can't place it, though.'

'He's part of the city's folklore, leastways the underside of the folklore. His is a name that will have cropped up in conversation with your mates from time to time. He's a knifeman. Tuesday Noon will certainly know of him, hopefully he'll know where to find him. Don't approach him. Have a look at the file on Toni Durham, by way of caution.'

'Who?'

'Toni Durham. She was murdered ten days ago and her body was found last night. She's linked in with Stephanie Craigellachie. Glance at the file and apprise yourself and look at the photographs of her body. It's as well to be aware of the sort of mess that Jimmy "the Rodent" Purdue can make of his victims in case you may feel inclined to feel his collar on your own. Where's King, do you know?'

'Came in and went out again. Said something about having to trace a scratcher.'

'Ah yes.' Donoghue smiled. 'Good man is King, doesn't hang about. Well, I'll let you get back to your newspaper, Montgomerie.'

Malcolm Montgomerie stood and reached for his jacket.

'Aye, I remember that one,' said the scratcher, holding the photograph at arm's length. 'I really mind that one. How could I forget a job like that.'

'How indeed?' said King drily, though he was pleased that the scratcher seemed serious. A flippant attitude would have been hard for him to take. 'When did you do this?'

'See, it's July. It was the winter, say about six months ago.' The man was in his fifties, thought King, probably older, but had retained a trim figure. It was his bald head and silver hair just above each ear that dated him. The scratcher handed the photograph to King, who slipped it in the orange internal mail envelope he used to carry the print.

'It was when there was snow and ice about, say February.'

'Six months,' King repeated. In his experience six months was a convenient time period and had in the past been used when six weeks or on one particularly memorable occasion eighteen months would have been more accurate reporting. But on this occasion, King reasoned, the unsolicited reference to the weather at that time leant a certain credibility to the man's statement.

'About that,' said the man, the scratcher. His studio was at the rear of a house in Bridgeton, dimly lit and smelling of damp. In the studio was a chair evidently for the tattooist, a reclining chair for the customer, a fearsome-looking antique drill and a table on which lay pots of dye. The cloth on the table was badly stained with the spillage of dye over the years and the pots themselves were caked with dried colouring. King felt that the whole room must be crawling with AIDS and Hepatitis B virus. It would be a quick and a telling phone call to the Environmental Health Department when he got back to the office, no matter how cooperative was the scratcher.

'Did she come alone?'

'Yes.' The man seemed to be reliving the memory. 'Had to do it on the floor, you know, the tattoo, had to have her lie down. It was cold then, wintertime, she shivered and seemed uncomfortable when the drill began to bite, but she stuck it out. She said she wanted "I belong to Dino" tattooed right here—' the man laid the edge of his hand on his groin —'and that's what she got. Never forget that, bonny-looking lassie, comes in out of the rain and says what she says. I couldn't believe it. When do you want it done, says I. Right now, says she. I'll need your clothes off, hen, says I, bottom half anyway, so she steps out of her jeans and briefs calm as you please. I put an old coat down on the floor, best I could offer, and I says, you'll need to lay down, hen, so down she went. She shivered a lot and made a wee cry out now and then, tattooing can be painful and where she had it done, well, it had to be uncomfortable to say the least.'

'To say the least,' King echoed. 'How long did it take?'

'Best part of two hours.'

'Brave girl.'

'She was that,' said the scratcher. 'She had a lot of grit about her.'

'How much did you charge her?' It occurred to King that Stephanie Craigellachie hadn't got a large amount of cash to spare, and that a tattoo is a luxury for anyone.

'Funny you should say that,' said the man.

'Oh?'

'She didn't.'

'Meaning?'

'Meaning I finished it, I examined it, said it was good, said that it would be fifty quid.'

'Fifty?'

'Well, I have to meet my overheads.'

'So then what?'

'So then she says I haven't a penny. She said that, I haven't a penny, sorry sir, I haven't a penny.'

'And what did you do?'

'I was ready to give her a good doing. Anyway, she says, I can pay you in kind, that's how she put it. So I looked at her, she was a bonny girl, so we struck a deal, she was to come round one night a week for three weeks and stay for an hour each time. Well, I stay alone, I never married and a lady from time to time is nice. She leaves, she pulls her jeans on and leaves. I'm not daft, I think I've been had and I don't expect to see her again, but the next night she's at my door at seven o'clock and stayed until the back of eight and it was a good sixty minutes, she put everything into it. She came round twice more after that, good as gold she was, honoured her word and paid her debt. I didn't get to know anything about her, but she was a person of quality, a lady underneath those clatty clothes. It didn't seem to fit.'

'How so?'

'Well, somebody that has herself tattooed like that, I'd say they were a bit dotty, soft in the head, not the sort of person to honour their word.'

'She probably was a little mad,' said King. 'The integrity of the mentally ill is a well-documented phenomenon.'

'Was?'

'Was,' said King. 'I'm afraid she was murdered just the other day there.'

'Oh my.' The man sank back against the table. 'So young.'

CONDITION PURPLE   145

'Did she say who Dino was?'

'No, never mentioned him, just spelled out his name so I got it right.'

'So she told you it was the name of a man?'

'Yes, she said "his name".'

'I see,' said King. 'She didn't say why she was doing this?'

The man shook his head. 'Really, she didn't.' The man paused. 'No, sir, she didn't.'

'Mr King or "Officer" will do,' said King, who hated being called "sir".'

'Well, anyway she didn't. Never talked about him or about herself for that matter. She talked about what was going on, asked about my business, polite lassie, never spoke about herself or her background, never said where she stayed, just came out of the night, kept her word, and went back into the night. Nice girl. She had a strange lost look about her. Sad eyes.'

'Sad eyes?'

'See me, Mr King, I'm like you, I'm in the people business. My business is direct contact with people, see all types in here, from hard men to totty wee boys just finished school, and I've had hard eyes, cold eyes, sad eyes, happy eyes, warm eyes and that girl had sad eyes. I don't know who Dino is or was but that was a lonely lassie, Mr King, a very lonely lassie.'

Big Jim Loughram worked Vice. He enjoyed a handsome, balanced face, his hair was beginning to thin, a 'beer gut' was just developing but he still cut a dash in pinstripe. He had eyes which said he knew of the ugliness of life, but his manner, Donoghue found, was the manner of a gentleman.

Loughram said, 'The Black Team?'

'You might know them by a different handle.' Donoghue crossed his legs and took out his pipe.

'Not in here, if you don't mind.' Loughram nodded

politely and good-humouredly to a No Smoking sign on the wall of his office.

'Of course.' Donoghue slipped his pipe into his jacket pocket.

'The Black Team? Enlighten me.'

So Donoghue enlightened him.

'I confess I didn't know that it was organized now,' said Loughram. 'Thirty- to forty-year-old women who no longer make money mugging the fifteen, sixteen- and seventeen-year-olds is as old as the game itself, but this is the first time I've heard of any organization being put into it. Usually it happens when a young girl bumps into an older woman who has had a bad night and it's a question of right, hen, down you go, thank you very much, you can earn it again in a couple of hours, I can't, so it's mine, and don't get angry because you'll be doing it yourself in ten years' time.'

'Fifteen-year-olds?' said Donoghue.

Loughram nodded. 'Fifteen is not uncommon, there's nothing you can do if a fifteen-year-old wants to go on the street. We lift them when we see them, but as often as not they've got a mate keeping the edge so they clear the pitch before we can grab them. If you want ages to worry about try fourteen, thirteen and even twelve.'

'Twelve!' Donoghue's own daughter was just nine years of age.

'Youngest known yet was a twelve-year-old Asian girl. I don't wish to be racist but Asian girls are very vulnerable. I've visited the sub-continent and I can tell you that Indian women are treated like horseflesh from an early age. Asians bring their cultural values with them when they relocate in the United Kingdom, just as British migrants to Australia carry our culture with them. So we found this twelve-year-old girl "servicing", as it's said, "servicing" the men in her extended family plus a few neighbours, she was being rented out by her father—her own father, mind. The girl was taken into care.'

'Of course.'

'But you're a cop yourself, and you know fine well that for every one we find, there's ten we don't find. But back to the Black Team: all I can say is that we haven't heard of them.'

'We'll be going out and talking to the ladies again tonight,' said Donoghue. 'If we hear anything of significance we'll let you know.'

'Thanks, but it's not Vice, strictly speaking. That's probably why we haven't logged anything about them. I mean, if they're controlling the girls, that's Vice, but if they're mugging them, that's just uncomplicated theft.'

'That's a fair point.' Donoghue nodded. 'Now the second question is, what do you know about Glasgow's other film industry?'

'What?'

So Donoghue told Loughram about Toni Durham's flat, the basement therein and the equipment in the basement.

'Wow,' said Loughram.

'I've had a preview of the videos,' said Donoghue, 'just to see if they can shed any light on the murder inquiries. They haven't so far. The content is heavy duty pornography and of course we'll be handing the tapes to you.'

'Thank you. Small studios like the one you describe are discovered from time to time and offensive material is seized. All that happens is that they shut down and open up again somewhere else. The tapes they make are copied and that's part of the operation we haven't yet found. Somewhere, maybe, in fact most probably abroad, is a room with banks and banks of sophisticated video-recording equipment that can enable a master tape to be reproduced at high speed. If we can locate that part of the operation we can shut any such operation down. The problem for us is that most tapes go for export, there's a bigger market for pornography on the continent than there is in the United Kingdom.'

'I see.'

'So it's our guess that the reproduction is done abroad. It's easier to smuggle one tape to Scandinavia than two thousand.'

'Of course. Now do you know of any name connected with the pornography industry in Glasgow? We're particularly interested in a guy called Purdue.'

'Purdue?'

'Sometimes called "the Rodent".'

Loughram shook his head. 'Rings no bells. What does he look like?'

'He's well into his fifties, stocky character, drives a black Mercedes, scarred face, going bald so he grows his hair long at one side and combs it across the top of his head.'

Loughram stood. He walked across the office floor to a filing cabinet, opened a drawer and lifted out a file. He took a photograph from the file and handed it to Donoghue.

'That's the man,' said Donoghue quietly. The photograph showed Purdue walking in the street.

'Shot through a telephoto lens,' said Loughram, resuming his seat. 'We think he's behind a lot of vice in this town, the massage parlours particularly, and maybe he's into films as well. We know him as "Fingers" McLelland.'

'Fingers?' said Donoghue.

'Apparently he's good at breaking people's fingers when he's trying to get a point across.'

'We know him as James "the Rodent" Purdue. He's a knifeman, already served ten years in the slammer for murdering a girl when he was a young man. If you have to approach him, approach him with caution, but I'd like to talk to him about something a little more substantial than immoral earnings.'

'Which is?'

'Double murder.'

'Substantial enough.'

'Where does he live?'

'We don't know.' Loughram shrugged his shoulders.

'He's seen around, we've never had to put a tail on him for any reason, we know him because he keeps cropping up in all the wrong places.'

'Well, from now on if you happen to see him just stick to him like a pair of wet denims until we can get there. Better still, just lift him for us.'

'Pleasure,' said Loughram. 'We see him once or twice a week, then he disappears for a month or two. We have the impression that he stays locally, by which we mean the Glasgow environs, but it's just an impression.'

Donoghue thanked Loughram. He took his hunter out of his waistcoat pocket as he walked down the corridor. It was 12.17. Perhaps a stroll to Kelvingrove Park and a light lunch in the café that he had recently discovered?

CHAPTER 9

Thursday, 12.30–21.30 hours

Montgomerie thought that he never changes, this man, he just doesn't change. Not only does Tuesday Noon not change, but Montgomerie couldn't even imagine him growing up, looking at him, gnarled face, whiskers, scars, a hot rasping breath. Could he ever have been a wee boy running home from school? Could he ever have been a young man experimenting with alcohol and chasing women? It was hard for Montgomerie to associate the growth process with Tuesday Noon, it was as if he had always been like this and would always be so. And he never changed his habitat, always here in sawdust of the Gay Gordon where the chairs and tables are chained to the floor, where young men and women openly shoot up, where they say a revolver and six rounds of ammunition can be bought over a table for cash and no questions asked, where the colour television sits high on the wall with both the colour and volume turned up too high. Right then it was racing from Newmarket.

His manner doesn't change either. Montgomerie had placed a glass of Teacher's in front of him and Tuesday Noon picked up the glass with weatherbeaten red hands with short stubby fingers and sank the drink in one. Neat. Then, as always, the glass was put back on the table and pushed across towards Montgomerie, sliding easily on the spilled alcohol, with as always Tuesday Noon looking at Montgomerie.

'You know you never change.'

'Aye, Mr Montgomerie.'

'You've no news for me yet?'

The sun streamed in through the window and the interior of the Gay Gordon, greenhouse-like, was hot and stale, smelling strongly of unwashed bodies and alcohol vapour. Nevertheless, it was more honest in Montgomerie's view than many of the modern Glasgow bars which subscribe to the 'casino principle', no natural light, no clocks, soft dark furnishings, dim lights, everything geared to creating an illusion of unreality to assist punters to part with their money all the more readily. Reality comes hard on closing time, when the burglar bell is switched on, the lights turned up and the bar staff start yelling. Then comes reality, the night, cold and wet or the white nights of summer, the gutter. Montgomerie glanced at his watch: 12.30, better make this quick, Malcolm, got to tear over to the Long Bar in time to pick up Collette when she finishes the first part of her split shift.

'I've been keeping my ears open. Nothing about the girl who was stabbed. Nothing, not a thing that wasn't in the *Record*.'

'You're not pulling your weight, Tuesday.'

'I need time. I mean, it was only Tuesday that it happened. Just forty-eight hours past. Rumours and whispers need time to spread.'

'Well, keep listening. In the meantime tell me what you know about a man called Purdue? Also known as "the Rodent". Mean anything?'

Tuesday Noon caught his breath.

'So it does mean something to you?'

'Aye.'

Montgomerie took a photograph from his jacket pocket. 'That the guy?'

'Aye. He's been around for years. He's changed his name.'

'Oh?'

'Aye.' Tuesday Noon clicked his tongue. 'He's calling himself Fingers something.'

'Fingers something?'

'Aye. He's not a nice man.'

'Very few people we are interested in are nice, Tuesday.'

'See, I hadn't heard of him for some time, he was a hard wee sewer rat in his day, but he came up in the world, still hard but he doesn't stay in rat holes no more. I knew him by sight, I heard he was a pure swine in the drink, without the drink he's just a swine. Then I clocked him in a bar, I asked a guy, the guy says, "Aye, that's Purdue, only now he's Fingers Mc-something."'

'Mc-something?'

'Aye. He's called Fingers on account of what he does to the fingers of people he doesn't take to.'

'I see.' Montgomerie stood. Went to the gantry and brought back another measure of Teacher's. 'I'm all ears, Tuesday.'

'Stays out of town,' said Tuesday, bringing the glass back down on to the table and, never changing, pushing it hopefully across towards Montgomerie. 'Not too far out, Strathblane, Fintry, that way out, they sort of places, places I've never been. Got a big house, fenced off all round with Rottweilers in the grounds.'

'Rottweilers?'

'Aye. They say Rottweilers eat Dobermans.'

'So I hear,' said Montgomerie. 'So where does he hang out when he's on the town, I mean now that he's come up in the world?'

'I saw him in a bar down by the Cross but he was only in there because he was looking for a guy. I hear he likes a flutter, so you could try the casinos.'

'OK, Tuesday, you've earned your crust after all.' Montgomerie handed him a five-pound note.

As Montgomerie left the pub through the narrow double doors he glanced over his shoulder and saw Tuesday Noon, already at the gantry, waving the note at the barman.

Outside, Montgomerie breathed the relatively clean air pushing out the stale air he'd accumulated inside the Gay Gordon. It was a hot day, the housing scheme on the hilltop gleamed in the sun, panes of glass winked at him, and over to his right the sun made the old stonework of Port Dundas glow. He walked towards Charing Cross and stopped at the phone-box close to St George's tube station. He phoned in Tuesday Noon's information and asked the constable on the switchboard to read his message back to him: Purdue, now known as Fingers Mc-something, domicile Fintry/Strathblane area, approach with caution because of dangerous dogs; Fingers thought to visit casinos; information for Inspector Donoghue as soon as possible. Then he put the phone down. Lucky, he thought, that the Inspector was out to lunch, otherwise, following the transmission of information, Donoghue, Montgomerie knew, would inevitably ask, 'What are your movements now?' and finding that Montgomerie had no immediate task, there would follow a summons back to P Division and an immediate task would be allocated. Donoghue, Montgomerie thought, is someone else who doesn't change.

The city was baking, cars with soft tops had them buttoned down, girls looked cool in summer cotton, guys sat in doorways, stripped to the waist, pulling on cans of lager. Montgomerie strode up Great Western Road with long, effortless strides, his jacket slung over his shoulder, enjoying as he had since he was seventeen the admiring glances of women as they passed. He was making for Kelvinbridge, for the Long Bar and a delicate pretty thing who would be just finishing up for the morning. Montgomerie had in fact a hard and a firm idea of his movements that afternoon, largely helped by Collette and her Thursday split.

In a sudden penetrating icicle of realization Elka Willems saw that being torn apart by James 'the Rodent' Purdue, also known as 'Fingers', was one of the few acts of passion that Toni Durham had experienced. She said so to Richard King.

'What do you mean?' The chubby, bearded cop looked up from the desk drawer in which he was rummaging.

'Well, look at this flat,' she said, glancing round her from where she sat on the settee. She put down a folder of papers beside her. 'There's no life here in this house, there never has been any life here, look at it, wall to wall carpets, three settees, full-length drapes over the windows, hardwood furniture, all dead. It's like being in a furniture shop. It's a place to work in, to eat in, breathe in and nothing else, and all that sweating and groping that went on in the basement in front of the cameras, that was just mechanical. No passion there at all. And look at these letters, just bills, letters from the garage, letters from solicitors, letters from businessmen, all typed on headed notepaper, not a personal handwritten letter among them.'

King nodded. 'Point taken.' He returned his attention to the contents of the drawer.

'So when this animal clawed her open, well, what I mean is she had no passion in her life but the poor wretched girl had it in her death.'

'You're feeling sorry for her?'

'Yes.' Elka Willems crossed one slender leg over the other. She had very feminine movements, even to King, who had eyes for no one except his beloved Quakeress wife. Even to King, the unflattering serge skirt and crisp white blouse of Elka Willems's uniform did nothing to hamper a femininity which she exuded from every pore. She definitely had that little bit extra which is difficult to define and which some women have and some women have not. Even to King.

'That's a dangerous emotion,' he said. 'Remember the importance of retaining professional detachment. Toni Durham had to be a hard woman to survive like this without any emotion. Try to look at it that way. If you had to pinch pennies in a damp single end and you live without emotion, then yes, then you are a tragic case. But if you live like this, velvet curtains, deep pile carpets, without any emotion, then that's a decision that you're taking. Frankly, I don't feel anything for her. If you ask me she put folding green above everything and she may well have sucked Stephanie Craigellachie into this spider's web and look what happened to her, a knife in her throat in some downtown alley.'

'Since you put it like that.' Elka Willems picked up the folder of pages.

Moments later King said, 'Gold dust.' He held an address book in his hands.

Donoghue turned the pages of the addressbook. Elka Willems and Richard King sat patiently in front of his desk as he did so. They heard the occasional page 'crack' as Donoghue methodically leafed through the book. 'Either it's new,' he said, 'or she didn't use it much. My guess is that she didn't use it much. There's hardly any entries. The two that we need are here, though. Did you see them?'

'Yes,' said King. 'I glanced at it. Noticed an entry for "home", just a telephone number, a Springburn number, I think. That was the only one I could see that might be of use to us. But you say there's two?'

'Yes, a useful phone number here against the name Fingers.'

'Fingers?'

'There's been developments while you have been out, Richard. I paid a call on our friends in the Vice Squad who were able to inform us that our prime suspect—'

'Purdue.'

'The one and the same, is also known as Fingers McLelland. When I returned to the office after lunch there was a message from Montgomerie, informing that Purdue is also known as Fingers something, has an address north of the city, lives in a house guarded by a pack of Rottweilers. Fingers, also known as Purdue, is apparently to be seen in the city's casinos. He enjoys a flutter, so we are informed.'

'So I assume we plan to lift him in the city rather than at home?

Donoghue reached for the phone on his desk. He dialled 9 for an outside line and then 100 for the operator. 'You assume correctly, Richard.' He paused. 'Ah yes, DI Donoghue here, P Division at Charing Cross. Can I speak to the controller, please? Thank you . . . Yes, controller, DI Donoghue, P Division here, we're making inquiries in connection with a serious crime. I have two telephone numbers here, if I give them to you could you identify their location? Yes, of course you can call back.' He read out the two telephone numbers and replaced the phone. He lit his pipe. 'Taken any holidays yet?'

'Crete, sir,' said Elka Willems. 'Very enjoyable.'

'Not yet, sir,' said King. 'We've pored over the brochures but haven't booked anything. I feel guilty about taking holidays when there's so much work to do on and in the house, such as the shelves I've been promising Rosemary for months now, I've got so far as buying the wood, and it's still leaning where I left it, she hasn't complained, she never does. We might grab some winter sun in November.'

'I remember when we were first married, house had to come first, didn't have a proper holiday until three years after we had moved in, we didn't miss one either. It was a very happy period. Now we let our children choose the holidays, we give them the brochures and they choose the location on the basis of the pictures. Last year it was Greece because Louise went ga-ga over a photograph of a donkey on a hillside. This year we're going to Malta because after all the squabbling they finally agreed that they both liked the brightly-coloured boats in Valetta harbour. My wife—'

Then the phone rang.

'Donoghue.' He listened. 'Yes, put her through, please . . . Yes, hello, madam, thank you for being so prompt . . .' Donoghue picked up his pen and scribbled on his pad. 'Thank you, that's a great help.' He replaced the receiver. 'Well,' he said, 'Mr and Mrs Durham live in Galloway Street, Springburn. If you'd like to go and do the necessary. Never easy, but it has to be done. Try and dissuade them from viewing the body. We are certain of the identity.'

'Very good, sir.'

'For myself, as a privilege of rank, I shall take a drive into the country to see how close I can get to the Rottweilers.'

Richard King and Elka Willems climbed the concrete stair of the flats at Galloway Street. The contents of a large communal dustbin which stood beneath a refuse chute had been incinerated, the flames had scorched the wall at the side of the stair up to a height of twenty feet. The cops stepped on to the landing which stretched the length of the street and which was broken up at intervals by iron railings, and padded along the heavy-duty rubber matting that formed the surface of the walkway. Below them in the street, boys kicked a ball about, two men leaned over the open bonnet of a car. A woman laboured with a heavy shopping-bag in each hand. King and Willems walked along the gallery until they came to a door with 'Durham' engraved on a tartan background just above the doorbell. King pressed the bell and, in doing so triggered an electronic rendering of 'Waltzing Matilda' which played loudly in the interior of the flat.

The front door was immediately wrenched open by an angry man. He didn't say anything, he didn't do anything but both cops felt his anger. It was in his eyes, the accusationary, aggressive coldness of his look. Similarly both cops recognized the pent-up resentment and fury of the type so common in prison inmates. Elka Willems's skin crawled and she was very very glad she hadn't come alone.

'Mr Durham?' King asked, holding the man's stare. 'Police.'

'I can tell that,' he snarled, rather than spoke.

'We're calling in connection with your daughter, Toni. May we come inside?'

The two cops found Mrs Durham to be the opposite of her husband. She was small and timid and sat hunched on the settee. She whimpered as she recognized the uniform of a WPC.

'What is it?' growled the man.

'I'm afraid we have some bad news, Mr Durham,' said King, again holding the man's stare. 'I'm afraid that I have to inform you that Toni is dead.'

Mrs Durham let out a piercing wail and ran from the room. Elka Willems followed her.

'Leave her be,' said Durham.

Elka Willems paused, turned and glared at the man and continued to follow the woman. The man flinched with anger.

'So what happened?' He turned on King.

'We believe she was murdered,' said King.

'Murdered, ha!'

'You don't seem so concerned, sir.'

'Should I be?' The man dominated the room, by his sheer overpowering personality as much as by his bulk. He was a man who bristled with cleanliness, neatly pressed shirt and trousers, polished shoes. The house was neat, tidy, a household where everything was kept in its place, including, thought King, the women. Durham squared up to King, balancing his weight evenly on both feet, pulling his shoulders back, and slightly bending his elbows. He was just one or two movements away from throwing a punch at the thing who had upset the order of the household.

'So what happened?' he said again. 'Are you going to tell me?'

'She was murdered.'

'You said that, you already told me that, and look at the effect you had on her.' The man nodded behind him towards the bedroom door from which a low wailing sound was emanating. 'She did that as well, our Toni, she was a rotten little bitch, she did that to her, made her upset.'

'She died about ten days ago.'

'So that's why she didn't call this time, this time she had some excuse.'

'Excuse?'

'Excuse for not calling her. She was dead so she had an excuse, but not for the other times, week in, week out, we never get a phone call, never get a letter, look at the house, have a good look at it. There's not many girls grow up in a home as good as this, see the hours I had to put in to buy this furniture, see that velvet wallpaper, all that crawling under people's cars I did just to build a home they could be proud of and she thinks she can walk out at the age of seventeen and not see us except maybe once or twice a year. And when she does come it's smart clothes and a fancy motor. Never told us what she did, said she was some kind of personal assistant.' The man's voice rose steadily. 'She had two sisters, I did right by them, was a proper father and they turned out all right, got married, had kids, what else do you want for your daughters and as soon as possible, so they don't have any chance to get into trouble. Leave school at sixteen, marry at eighteen, first child at twenty. That's how it should be. The first two did it like that, just like they should, but our Toni she got away with too much, let her off too often, her mother wanted it that way, said I was too hard on the others, but she was wrong, I was right. If she'd have let me bring up Toni properly she wouldn't have ended up like this. Let my woman stay upset, she brought it on herself. I knew she was wrong.' By this time the man's voice was echoing in the house, utterly drowning the sound from within the bedroom.

Donoghue drove out of Glasgow. He enjoyed the drive, out towards the Campsies, Verdi on the hi-fi, sun roof wound open, the Rover behaving impeccably. Out here, he thought, one could breathe, and breathe in Scotland at her most beautiful; in the summer.

He parked his car in the pub car park at Strathblane and strolled with his jacket slung over his shoulder up a narrow road which led ultimately to Lennoxtown. Within five minutes he was well clear of the village and out to where the houses stood in their own grounds, clearly fenced off from each other, surrounded by well-tended gardens and cypress trees. Two, sometimes three, cars stood in the driveway. Donoghue eventually came upon the house identified by British Telecom as having the phone number written against the entry 'Fingers' in Toni Durham's crisp and almost void address book. The house was surrounded by a high wire fence and at frequent intervals along the fence at adult eye level were signs in bold red paint which read 'Dangerous Dogs'. Donoghue stepped off the roadway and approached the gate.

Nothing moved. The house was in silence. The gardens quite still, not even a breath of wind to disturb the shrubs. He looked again at the house, it was large, white-painted with a roof of black tile. He shook the gate.

A dog barked.

Then another. Barking with a deep, menacing tone. One, then two dogs approached at the far end of the drive, black

and brown animals with wide shoulders and powerful jaws.
Rottweilers. They ran down the drive towards Donoghue.
Two more followed. Four dogs in all pounded down the
driveway and ran at the gate, throwing themselves, clawing
and snarling at the fencing, slavering at the mouth with
massive claw-like paws. Some dogs.

A middle-aged and overweight man in corduroy trousers
and garden boots walked from behind the garage and stood
staring down the drive, looking at Donoghue. Donoghue
looked back. The distance between the two men was too
great to enable them to communicate even by shouting but
they stood there fixing each other's stare. Then Donoghue
stepped back from the gate and the growling, snarling pack
of dogs and turned to walk on, but not before he noticed a
sneer grow on the lips of the gardener; another city smoothie
out to clear the tubes and getting more than he bargained
for.

'Where are you going, Dino? You've just come in from your
work and I've made a nice quiche for you. Tomorrow it's
Friday, I want to be taken out to look at the flowers. I mean,
it's the end of the week, but you just dash in and out and
I've got the good china out for your tea. When will you be
back, an hour, two hours? I'll make some more tea when
you get back in.' He gripped the steering-wheel. God forgive
me, but you bitch, you damn bitch, whistle, won't you,
please just break into song, you're almost there, if I deliber-
ately annoy you you might just do it, your voice goes through
me, it goes down my spine like the sound of a wet finger
being drawn across glass goes down my spine. Make as
much tea as you like when you like, with your pretty, dainty
little hesitant movements.

'I can see what Montgomerie's grass meant about the dogs,'
said Donoghue. 'There was a tall and hefty fence between
us but I was scared none the less.'

'I'll bet, sir.' King sipped his coffee. 'I've heard of Rottweilers, came to the United Kingdom with the Roman Legions, I believe.' Montgomerie pulled on his pipe and glanced at his hunter, 17.00 hours, a nice point to begin to wrap up the day's work and allocate tasks for the back shift and the graveyard shift. A suspect has been identified, a warrant for arrest issued, present location unknown. 'How did you get on with Toni Durham's next of kin?'

'Her father is a pure animal,' said King and went on to explain what he meant.

'I see.' Donoghue drained his mug and placed it on his desk. 'I see.'

'So what's on the agenda, sir?'

'I was chewing over that question,' Donoghue replied. 'I think the only thing we can do is to watch the house and the casinos until we see Purdue and then bring him for questioning. We'll need overwhelming numbers when we do move.'

'Firearms, sir?'

Donoghue shook his head. 'I don't think so, Richard. Purdue is a knifeman, a dozen drawn truncheons will suffice, use a sledgehammer to crack a nut, prevents unnecessary violence. We have to pounce before he knows what is happening, snap the cuffs on and seize control.'

'Hope it's as easy as that. Do we have a warrant?'

'Yes. It was sworn this afternoon. I think all we can do now is wait for him to surface, could be a long wait, he's a bit of a fly-by-night.'

King smiled. 'I think we can seize initiative, sir. I mean what if Sid should phone wanting to speak to Fingers?'

Donoghue smiled. 'On you go, Sid.'

King picked up the phone and dialled 9 for an outside line and then dialled the number of Purdue's residence in Strathblane as Donoghue read it out from the file.

The phone rang out.

'No answer,' said King.

'Hang in there,' said Donoghue. 'At least the gardener is at home.' So King hung in. Eventually the phone was answered. 'Yes,' said a gruff voice.

'It's Sid,' said King.

'Sid?'

'Yes. Fingers told me to phone him when I got into town. We've got some business to talk over.'

'He's not here,' said the voice. 'He's not due back from Germany until the end of the week.'

'That's tomorrow,' said King. 'It's Thursday evening now.'

'Aye, so it is. Sid, you say?'

'Aye.'

'I'll tell him you called. You could try again tomorrow.'

'Right.' King put the phone down. 'We have to watch all incoming flights from Germany, sir.'

'Germany?'

'Yes. From right now. He's returning any time now.'

'Right.' Donoghue snatched the phone and dialled the Airport Police. He spoke to them briefly and then replaced the phone. 'They'll check the passenger lists for all flights from Germany for a male McLelland or a male Purdue,' said Donoghue. 'But they'd like a photograph of our man as soon as possible.'

'Abernethy could do that, sir,' King said. 'He's coming on duty any time now. He could drive down to the airport with a copy.'

'Right, if you'd ask him, please, Richard.'

Then the phone rang. Donoghue paused and then picked it up, identified himself and listened, said, 'Thank you,' and replaced the receiver. 'Well, well, well,' he aid.

'Well, well, well?' King raised his eyebrows.

'That was the uniform bar. A lady of the street has just phoned us to inform us that there is a man walking up and down Blythswood Street asking for Stephanie Craigellachie, telling the girls that Dino is looking for her. And I was looking forward to getting home on time for once.'

'We have a terrible, terrible relationship,' said the man. 'We just seem to mince about being nice to each other because she can't conceive of any other way for a married couple to behave. It's like playing at dolls' houses for her. I know these things cut both ways and I suppose I'm partly to blame, but I can't see my own faults, like most people. We don't have a level that we can communicate on.' The man shrugged and took another cigarette from his packet. Donoghue extended his lighter. 'Thank you. On Friday evenings she wants me to take her for a walk to look at the wild flowers, I want to go to the hotel for a beer or two to unwind after the week's work. There's nothing wrong in wanting to go for a walk on Friday evenings and there's nothing wrong with having a drink after work on Friday, but there is something wrong in one wanting to do one and one wanting to do the other and still calling it a relationship. We are not married, we are two strangers living in the same house, sharing the same bed.'

Donoghue glanced out of the window. He liked the man, he liked his earthy honesty. He had decided very early in the piece that Dino Bawtry was of no interest to the police other than as a member of the public who was willing to give information. Dino Bawtry had been startled by the police officers, Richard King and two constables, but had after a few seconds' protestation willingly accompanied the officers to the police station. There he had taken the news of Stephanie Craigellachie's death very badly. Very badly indeed. It was some minutes before he was composed enough to continue the interview.

'Where does "Dino" come from?' Donoghue filled his pipe.

'Army days,' said Dino Bawtry. 'I was in the Royal Horse Artillery, Madras Troop, you don't get better than that.

There were three Davids in the same battery, so one was
Dave, the other was Davy, and I got Dino, simple as that
and the name has stuck down the years. I enjoyed the army,
lot of good blokes in the army, the nickname carries a lot of
good memories with it.'

'So how did you get to know Stephanie Craigellachie?'

'I was lonely. I suffered that awful form of loneliness that
can only happen in a so-called relationship. You know that
phrase, "my wife doesn't understand me": what it really
means is that you can't be yourself in your relationship and
in that case you're better off alone because you can be
yourself if you live by yourself. I dare say it's the same for
my wife, Theresa, I dare say she can't be herself either. The
obvious thing would be to separate but we are practising
Catholics. We have made vows and we both intend to keep
them. It doesn't follow from that that we are content. I
realized too late that Theresa is very naïve.'

Donoghue grunted, pulling and sucking on his pipe.

'I'm a businessman, I instal central heating systems in
folks' houses. I tend towards hard-headed cynicism and in
the beginning Theresa's big-mindedness was, I thought, a
good check and balance for me, but for many years now I
have accepted that her magnanimity is nothing less than
childlike naïvety. She just hasn't a clue about life. I think
that she was a perfectly behaved little girl who did what
was expected of her. When she reached the age of twelve
she sniffed at adolescence and decided she didn't like it and
became middle-aged and then waited for the rest of her
generation to catch up with her. It meant she never de-
veloped any sort of personality over and above being a
model of "proper" behaviour. So I did what many men
would do. I went up the Square. Or rather the streets round
the Square. The difference between me and most men who
go up the Square is that I had no interest in sex. I hadn't.
I went up to communicate with a female who was realistic
about life.'

'Realistic?' Donoghue was suddenly reminded of a drunken conversation he had had while at university, he and two friends debated with steadily slurring speech the number of different 'realities' that existed. Not surprisingly, there was no resolution to the dispute.

'It was just refreshing for me to talk to a female who wasn't naïve, to sit with a girl whose bodily movements are strong and positive instead of being retiring and delicate. Theresa, when she reaches for my plate at the end of dinner, will hesitate just a split second before she lifts it from the table. She wants to avoid snatching it, but I wish she would just grab it. That would make her real.'

'So I went up the Square to talk to some realistic women. Girls really, and you know, more often than not they are nice girls. A few hard-edged ones but mostly they're nice kids. They have a tough life so there's no naïvety on the street.'

'You don't have to tell me.'

'Eventually I met Stephanie. I became her guardian, a protector. I'd give her what money I could to get her off the street for a night or two but she was a heroin addict.'

'I know.'

'So I could afford to pay for her habit. I wouldn't have done anyway but I did what I could. I tried to persuade her to start a de-tox programme but she wouldn't, she needed that evil stuff. She started to tell me about her life, she had a terrible childhood. I was the father she never had, she was the daughter I never had.'

'I see.'

'She was what I believe is currently called an "abused child".'

'She grew up in foster care,' said Donoghue.

'I know, but there's foster care and foster care. Her foster home sounded like hell on earth. In an odd sense my wife might be happy there in that everything is perfect. It was a home I understood that was littered with delicate ornaments, little glass animals, cuckoo clocks, fish tanks with model castles inside. Stephanie wasn't part of even that, her foster parents dressed well and she was given a school uniform to keep up appearances, but in the house she had to wear charity shop cast-offs, because she was fostered.'

Donoghue caught his breath.

'Oh, it gets worse, Mr Donoghue. When her foster parents sat down to roast beef she stood at the table in front of beans on toast, because she was fostered. Their home was apparently lavishly furnished but Stephanie's room was threadbare, cheap furnishing and no form of heating even in the winter. Worse was the physical abuse: something went missing from the house and off would come the man's belt, and not a few times, she showed me once, even at the age of twenty-one she still had the white marks on the back of her legs where the buckle of his belt had broken her skin all those years ago.'

'Oh, that makes me very angry,' said Donoghue quietly.

'Doesn't it. Then there was the verbal abuse, getting called a "slag" from the age of twelve, for example. The foster home was in Bearsden but she was bussed to school in Possilpark.'

'Because she was fostered.'

'That's it. And you know what Possilpark and Saracen are like, a hotbed of drugs.'

'I know fine.'

'So Stephanie at the age of sixteen years was convinced she was worthless and had a head full of problems, and so when somebody gave her a bag of white powder and said, "If you want your problems to go away, try this," she did.'

'So she was a heroin addict at sixteen.'

Dino Bawtry nodded. 'And who could blame her? Eventually she worked the street, came by way of petty larceny, shoplifting, breaking into cars, and when she hadn't got money she sat in her miserable bedsit doubled up with cramps and smelling of vinegar.'

'Vinegar?'

'Apparently she bought heroin in a soluble solution in which it was "cut" with vinegar. She used to inject it, puncturing herself in her neck and groin as well as her arms. If she cold turkey'd the smell of vinegar would come out of the pores of her skin. Once she bit through the skin of her finger, she was so strung out.'

'How long have you known her?'

'Going on a year. In that time, see, all the offers I had made to help her, but she had to come off the heroin, she couldn't do it. Even though she hated the street, hated herself, hated what she was doing she just wouldn't leave go. In a sense it was too easy, she was new and young and attractive, she could earn money. That caused her problems in itself.'

'The Black Team, you mean.'

'That's not a name I've heard of, Mr Donoghue.'

'It's apparently a group of older women who mug the younger ones.'

'Yes, she told me about them, I didn't know they were called that. She was rolled on a couple of occasions and had to stay out until five or six o'clock the following morning, working the casinos, mostly Chinese men at that time of day, she said they can be real rough handlers. After that she went home half way through each evening and deposited her earnings so if she was rolled she would only lose half a night's money.'

'Sensible. Did she work each evening?'

'Well, she was a smack head, she had to. You can always tell which girls are the heroin addicts, they are the ones who shiver in doorways wearing next to nothing when there's snow on the ground or the sleet is driving down, I've seen them standing there on Christmas night and Ne'er day night. The girls who come out in the summer two or three evenings a week, they're casuals, looking for pocket money. I couldn't make up my mind about the casuals. I couldn't help seeing them as exploiting as much as they were exploited. But Stephanie and girls like her . . .' Dino Bawtry shook his head. 'I mean, they have no choice.'

Donoghue pulled gently on his pipe.

'So Stephanie and I got to know each other, we met during the day and I bought her meals, she was emaciated and didn't eat properly. So then she thanked me. It's unbelievable, but it's true, she thanked me in the only way she knew. All that she thought herself to be was a body to be used by men so she had herself tattooed, but tattooed on her groin. She had "I belong to Dino" tattooed on her groin. She told me. I never saw it, I didn't want to see it.'

'We saw it at the post mortem,' said Donoghue. 'And we spoke to the tattooist who did the art work. She paid him with her body, she gave him three freebies.'

Again Dino Bawtry shook his head. 'She had such a low opinion of herself, she could not see herself as anything other than a piece of property to be owned or rented out. I kept on at her to at least get herself tested for AIDS, but she refused. I think she was frightened of being told that she had it.'

'It's not an uncommon attitude.'

'You know, Mr Donoghue, the thing that really reached me was that that life of hers, abandoned by her natural parents, sustained abuse of every kind in her foster home, heroin addiction at sixteen, no breaks in life, constant brushes with the law, a few weeks here and there in Cornton Vale hadn't hardened her. If she was a cold and a hard personality I could understand why, but she wasn't, she was warm, friendly, concerned for others. It was as if all the cruelty and exploitation and pain and humiliation could not destroy what was basically a good-natured personality. So then she wasn't on the street any more, no one knew where she had gone, and all I saw were the other girls and I thought: They all must have a background the same as

Stephanie's because even the casuals must have a profound sense of lack of worth to do what they do.'

Dino Bawtry took another cigarette from his packet and again Donoghue reached forward and proffered his lighter.

'Tell me,' said Donoghue, 'did Stephanie ever mention a girl called Toni Durham or a man called Fingers McLelland?'

'The man, no,' said Bawtry, 'not by name, anyway, but she did mention Toni by name. She makes films, so Stephanie said.'

'Blue movies,' said Donoghue. 'Stephanie was in some.'

'She told me she done something like that. She preferred it, it was safer than getting into cars with strange men.'

'Did she mention the name of her supplier.'

'No, not by name, just said that her supplier was female.' Then Bawtry looked startled. 'Yes, she did.'

'Oh!'

'Not by name, but it was that girl Toni Durham.'

'Really?'

'Yes, I remember, she said one time, she said, "My supplier's making me do films, I don't mind, it's safer than the street, I don't get money, I'm getting some smack."'

'Earlier she had told you that her supplier was female?'

'Yes. It seems she had to work the street to pay for heroin, and then her supplier offered her a part in a film for which she would be paid in powder.'

'Her supplier evidently being Toni Durham.'

'That's it. Do you know this Toni Durham? You going to nail her?'

'Somebody got there before us,' said Donoghue. 'It seems that the heroin Toni Durham gave to Stephanie wasn't Toni's to give. It belonged to a man called Fingers.'

There was a gentle tap on the door of Donoghue's office. Abernethy entered, young, very fresh-faced for a CID cop. He excused himself and asked to speak to the Inspector in private. In the corridor Abernethy informed Donoghue that the Airport Police had just telephoned. They had detained a man called McLelland who had arrived on the 18.00 hours flight from Hamburg.

'Ask them to hold him,' said Donoghue. 'We'll be right down.'

'We, sir?'

'We, sir. You and me, sir.'

The small man in the grey suit and red tie said, 'My client wishes to say nothing.'

'Who doesn't?' said Purdue, also known as McLelland. 'I'm my own man. I say what I please.' He was a short, stocky man, the same man in the photograph with Toni Durham and the black Mercedes, the same hard eyes, the same gouged face, lumps of dead skin and scars.

'Well then, I can be of no further assistance.' The solicitor stood. 'Gentlemen.'

'Good evening, sir,' said Donoghue.

A uniformed officer of the Airport Police opened the door and the solicitor left the room.

'See those guys,' said Purdue, 'see them.'

'So tell us why you did it?'

'Did what?'

'Little point in denying it,' said Donoghue. He felt unnerved in the presence of the man. The man's eyes were strange, they seemed to drill into him, cold, icy, scheming, cunning, they burned right through him and seemed to be burning into the wall behind Donoghue's head. He was glad of Abernethy's company, and of the company of two uniformed officers. 'Your fingerprints were in Toni Durham's blood.'

'So?'

'So you killed her.'

'So?'

'You're not denying it?'

Purdue shrugged his shoulders. 'Why deny it if you've got my dabs?'

'Why indeed?' said Donoghue. 'But it would be good to have a nice clean confession instead of hints and innuendoes. You realize that this makes three women that you have killed.'

'Three that you know of.'

'That we know of,' Donoghue echoed with a note of despair. 'The girl you did time for, Stephanie Craigellachie and Toni Durham.'

'Not bad, aye?' Purdue smiled.

Donoghue thought that Sussock was correct, this is a State Hospital case if ever there was one. Single to Carstairs Junction, please.

The door of the interview room opened. A sergeant of the Airport Police handed a note to one of the constables, who handed it to Donoghue. Donoghue read it and said, 'So that's why you went to Germany. We thought you were bringing pornography back.'

'I export the stuff,' said Purdue. 'Took a couple of master tapes for duplication over there.'

'You going to tell us what you brought back or are we going to tell you what we found in your suitcase?'

Purdue stared intently at Donoghue.

'Well, you can make it hard for yourself or easy. It's up to you. As it is, you are looking at two life sentences plus at least fifteen years for the contents of your suitcase.'

'So I make a bit of money. What's wrong with that?'

'Depends on how you do it. There's enough heroin in your suitcase to keep half of Glasgow supplied for a year.'

Purdue shrugged. 'Prove that it's mine. I think you've planted it.'

'We can prove that it's yours if we have to. I imagine it's got your dabs all over it. Probably under your fingernails as well.'

Purdue began to suck his fingers.

'You can do that as much as you like, it won't do you any good. It has to be dug out, but the fact that you saw fit to do that is significant.'

'OK, so you've nailed me. Where does that get you?'

'It gets me where I wanted to go as soon as I saw a knife sticking out of Stephanie Craigellachie's neck two days ago.'

'She shot her mouth off too much.'

'Why didn't you mutilate her like your other victims, especially Toni Durham?'

'She stole horse off me, Toni Durham. But I would have carved the Craigellachie girl if I hadn't been disturbed by the other women.'

'Other women?'

'The older dames that were going to roll the Craigellachie girl. See, she was standing at the entrance to the alley where she always stands and I was working up behind her. Then she starts backing into the alley, backing towards me, and as she does so she lobs her purse into the building site, but she keeps backing up. I mean, it couldn't be better so I waited for her to come on, I waited in a kind of backyard of some building. She came on backwards, I grabbed her, got her once in the throat, not neat, but I could tell by the blood that it was good enough.' The man suddenly seemed lost in thought and he smiled, he actually smiled at the memory.

'Get on with it!' Donoghue's patience was wearing thin.

'Aye, then I saw what she was backing away from, four women it was, older dames, one had a butcher's knife. They saw me, saw what I'd done. One screamed, they all ran, I ran. Anyway I was pushed for time. I had to catch the 10.00 p.m. flight to Hamburg. I had business to do in Hamburg.'

Donoghue shivered. The chilling matter-of-factness of it. 'And Toni Durham: you practically tore her apart?'

'Aye, I did a good job there right enough. A proper job. I was able to keep her alive long enough as well. She was still kicking when most of her blood was outside her.'

'So what did she do to annoy you, cough and not say she was sorry?'

'She lifted some horse that didn't belong to her, and she gave it away trying to blame Craigellachie, for one. For two, she brought that little bitch Craigellachie into the operation. Craigellachie had a fault, she couldn't keep her mouth zipped. Dangerous. She was useful, Toni was, but she was expendable.'

Malcolm Montgomerie left Collette's flat, he walked slowly, feeling relaxed and very, very satisfied. He walked to P Division police station, signed in and went up to the CID corridor. The corridor was deserted and there were no messages left for him in his pigeonhole. Donoghue was out, King was away, 'not back', Abernethy was 'out'. So he signed out also, 'not back', and went home thinking about a cool lager or two.

In Langside, in a room and kitchen, in a pine double bed Elka Willems lay awake, just looking at the ceiling and not thinking about very much at all. Beside her Ray Sussock lay in an awkward folded posture, slumbering, occasionally snoring. She let him sleep, not annoyed by his snoring, knowing he'd have to be woken soon, coaxed into life and pushed out into the night, grumbling and complaining, in order to make the graveyard shift on time.

Richard King let himself into the back door of his modest semi-detached house. His beautiful, beloved wife embraced him and pressed a mug of tea into his hands. Still in the kitchen, he picked up the wood he had bought the previous November in order to make shelves for her. He looked at the wood, felt the grain, looked along it to see that it was straight and true and then put it down again. He went into the living-room and helped Ian build a tower with his brightly-coloured plastic bricks.

In a house in Bearsden a well-dressed couple sat silently gazing into each other's eyes while a silver thing in the corner of the room went round and round and round.

Donoghue returned to his home in Edinburgh and in that hour before dusk, having left a good neighbour with their children, he and his wife strolled out arm in arm.

The thought struck him suddenly and forcibly that this was the first time that he and his lady had walked out in this manner.